Remembering the Bones

ALSO BY FRANCES ITANI

Deafening
Leaning, Leaning Over Water

FRANCES ITANI

REMEMBERING THE BONES

SCEPTRE

First published in Great Britain in 2008 by Sceptre
An imprint of Hodder & Stoughton
An Hachette Livre UK company

A CIP catalogue record for this title is available from the British Library

Hardback ISBN 978 0 340 95399 0
Trade Paperback ISBN 978 0 340 95402 7

Printed and bound by Clays Ltd, St Ives plc

Hodder & Stoughton policy is to use papers that are natural, renewable
and recyclable products and made from wood grown in sustainable forests.
The logging and manufacturing processes are expected to conform to the
environmental regulations of the country of origin.

Hodder & Stoughton Ltd
338 Euston Road
London NW1 3BH

www.hodder.co.uk

For Cam and Sam, arms crossed, love, love.
And for daughters of mothers everywhere.

And do you wonder
about your place under the huge
invisibly starry sky . . .
     as I do mine?
—Margaret Avison, "Relating"

One

THE RAVINE

ONE

Saturday, April 15, 2006

Georgie's suitcase is closed and locked, nothing valuable in the outer, zipped pockets, she's been warned. If you put locks on the outside, they'll be cut off in the name of security. That's what airport workers are entitled to do. They think nothing of hacking through the arm of a lock, or wrenching the tab off a zipper. You're better to keep every one of your belongings tucked deep inside your luggage. If you must stick something in the pockets, let it be a magazine, a pouch for dirty laundry, nothing more. Her daughter Case, frequent traveller, has given her a thorough briefing. So much briefing, Georgie feels stuffed with information. You'd think Case was the mother and she the child. But it's nothing more than Case's penchant to take charge, to direct; Georgie knows this as well as she knows the width of her own palm, the hinges of her own bones. Case owns a theatre, and she directs. That's what she knows how to do.

Georgie did pay attention to Case, but she doesn't pretend that she isn't nervous. She has flown only a few times and never

Leabharlanna Fhine Gall

by herself. Her first flight was when she and Harry took their Big Trip to Europe the year he retired. The following year, they flew to Seattle. They capitalized the words Big Trip in conversation because it had taken them a lifetime to save. It was easy to speak in capitals, one of the asides of a long marriage. She misses those small comforts—an eyebrow lowered, a tilt of the head. She misses his warm body next to hers in bed. But Harry is dead, has been dead for more than three years, and this is not the time to dip into loneliness and grief. She's facing a two-hour drive to the city airport, where she'll leave her car in the car park. She has already turned down Case's offer to drive her, knowing that Case is in the midst of rehearsals. And Georgie does not want anyone hovering. Haven't the Danforth women always been independent? She is on her way to Buckingham Palace, and she has decided to travel alone. The invitation allows *One spouse or One companion*, but whom does one bring to meet the Queen? Not her mother, Philomena, who lives at the Haven and is a hundred and three. Not her sister, who lives in Florida, though Georgie wonders if perhaps she should have invited Ally, after all. She misses her sister; hasn't seen her since Harry's funeral.

Too late to ask anyone now. And Georgie is the one who was born the same day as the Queen, April 21, 1926. Hasn't she always known she has a special shared birthday? Doesn't the invitation make that perfectly clear?

She turns out the lights and stands in shadows in her kitchen. Afternoon sun spills its warmth into her backyard and highlights the budding trees that edge the side of the ravine. Snow is gone; a crocus pushes through earth here and there. An unusually mild twenty-three degrees outside and good weather for flying, at least at the starting end. She has scattered peanuts for the jays and filled the feeders with sunflower seed and niger. She has watered her indoor ivies and the big jade, and checked the windows and doors. She'll be away ten days. There's bread in the freezer, butter in the butter dish, a tightly wrapped package of cheddar and two orange tomatoes. Enough for a sandwich when she gets back. She likes to plan; she won't have to shop immediately when she returns. She stares into the branches of the chokecherry tree at the back window. And with the lights out, catches a glimpse of her own reflection.

She's wearing her Austrian wool cardigan beneath a matching spring coat. Both are a soft, mossy green. Slacks, so she'll be comfortable on the plane overnight. Sensible shoes—doesn't want swollen feet in the morning. If she were to pick up the phone here in Ontario, England would be five hours ahead. By the time she gets there tomorrow, it will be more hours than that. Twenty maybe. And then subtract five. Who cares? She can't stop to figure it out. It's enough to know that she'll have to try to sleep on a plane that has been designed to fly the width of the Atlantic, west to east, and touch down on the outskirts of London in the early morning.

Hector Protector was dressed all in green
Hector Protector was sent to the queen

Shouldn't she gather up her things, walk out the front door, come back in, sit for a moment and then depart a second time? It's what characters in Russian novels do—to ward off ill fortune, to ensure a safe journey. But no, she has to get moving.

Case was at the house an hour ago to say goodbye. She gave her mother a hug and left a small gift bag stuffed with orange paper on the passenger seat of Georgie's car. "Don't look until you're in the air," she called back from the driveway. "You can carry it as hand luggage. See? It's not so big. Wait until you're over the ocean before you look inside." Then Case jumped into her own car and drove down the hill and into town, for rehearsal.

Georgie wonders if Harry, given his history—and if he were alive, which he isn't—would have agreed to accompany her on this trip. Didn't he refuse to include England when they planned their Big Trip? She missed Buckingham Palace then, and didn't complain. Now she has a second chance. The invitation from the Queen is tucked inside her new black purse, along with the P. D. James paperback she'll read in the airport. Everything is new, the purse with the leather shoulder strap that will leave her hands free to hand over her passport, to exchange currency, to hail a London cab. The blue dress is new; she drove to the city to find it—a two-hour trip like the one she is facing today. The dress is made of luxurious silk, round neck, pearl buttons on the cuffs, and is wrapped in folds of tissue paper, the last item to be packed. Her pearl necklace is not new but is in its case in the purse because it can't be trusted to airport security. Harry designed the necklace and strung the pearls himself, each and every pearl secured with a double knot. A long time ago.

What if the toe of her shoe gets caught in a palace rug and she falls flat on her face before the Queen? Will Charles be there and quickly grab her arm? Will Philip speak to her? Will she remember what to do? Will she have a chance to return to see the famous art collection? What if? What if? She checks one more time for tickets, pearls, sheets of protocol, which she'll review on the plane after she orders a glass of champagne. What an adventure! The invitation is there, too:

The Master of the Household has received Her Majesty's command to invite Mrs. Georgina Danforth Witley to a Lunch to mark the 80th Birthday of The Queen.

Ninety-nine men and women received the invitation, in all parts of Elizabeth's kingdom, every one born the same day. Georgie has been commanded to arrive between 12:30 and 1:00 p.m., Wednesday the 19th, because the event will be held two days before their actual birthday. She is allowing herself several days in London to recover from jet lag and do a little sightseeing before going to the palace. She wants to be rested, calm. She'll have five full days after the celebration, and will fly home the 25th. She wants to walk the streets of the ancient city and visit places she has read about all her life. She wants to sit tall in a London cab and drive past sites she has known only from photographs and her imagination: Marble Arch, Piccadilly, Downing Street, Big Ben. She'll walk through the Abbey and remember stories of kings and queens, explorers and poets. She'll run her hands over the bones or memorials of Handel and Hardy, Browning and Chaucer, the Brontës and Shakespeare. Her footsteps will echo over old stone. She'll have tea at Fortnum & Mason's and visit the Victoria and Albert Museum, the National Portrait Gallery, Dickens' house and the Tate. She'll buy a scarf of Liberty silk and she'll try to get a ticket for a play, and she'll run out of energy before she'll run out of things to do.

Georgie picks up her keys and passes the mahogany cabinet with the glass doors where she has stored the memorabilia she has collected from the time Elizabeth was a young princess painted by de László. In Georgie's miniature copy, the princess is holding a basket of flowers and wears a full, pale dress with a blue satin sash. Her hair is waved and tinted with gold, and the bones of her fingers are delicate and slender. There are also programs, postcards, *Maclean's* 1937 special Abdication issue—five cents a copy—which includes the "Message of Abdication" from King Edward VIII, and all of the speeches and proclamations that followed and broke so many hearts. There are maps of Royal visits, a Coronation matchbook stamped *Elizabeth R 1953*, and *The Princess Elizabeth Gift Book*, which finally became Georgie's when Ally and her husband, Trick, packed up and moved to Boca Raton. It's all there. It's all there in Georgie's collection. Even a Royal scrapbook from the forties, which Case found in an antique store in the city. Case teases Georgie about her collection, but that didn't stop her from making a contribution.

Georgie does not go out the door and come back inside to sit for a moment, the way the Russians do. They're so excitable, she thinks. They never stop talking, even when they do come back in and sit down. She hoists her suitcase into the trunk of the car, says a silent thanks that she's still fit enough to hoist things at all, climbs into the driver's seat and spots Case's gift on the seat beside her. She presses on the bag with two fingers and sees that it's something soft. She backs out—there are only four houses at the top of the ravine, so it's always quiet on her street—and heads the half-mile down the hill where she'll join the highway that leads out of town. As she rounds the first curve, she checks her wrist to be certain she hasn't forgotten her watch, the one with the wide gold strap. Because her attention is on her wrist, she allows the steering wheel to twist slightly to the right. In a split second, the right front wheel slips off the pavement. The moment the tire catches a depression in the shoulder, the entire car gives a jolt, and Georgie's hands clamp back onto the steering wheel.

But the car, with a mind of its own now, refuses to continue the curve. It has already nosed itself between a pair of striped railings that have been spaced to prevent this very thing from happening. The railings are meant to give warning, deflect danger, to keep wheels on pavement where they are absolutely supposed to be. But Georgie's car has neatly fit between end-posts, and now it is falling through space, silently at first, so that the event unfolds as if it is not to be believed. The car lands in the top branches of a large tree and then flips, and flips again, and brushes past another tree, and down and down.

Georgie has not cried out. Her mouth is open and then her teeth clench, and she holds tight even knowing that she cannot steer through air. Just as the car does its first somersault, her mind perceives the word *tree*. She has fallen sideways, but her eyes are open and her pupils dilate as if they are watching a slow-moving picture in which millions of dots have gathered for the sole purpose of shaping and reshaping themselves. Hundreds and thousands of leaves assemble and float by, the veins in each separate and distinct. An image drifts through memory, a long-ago childhood image of a glass-leafed ornament on an oak table. Tiny leaves, faceted and smooth, attach to filaments of copper wire. Miniature branches of threaded silk reach out, pale and soft as moss. A slender trunk nestles to a glass base and fits the curve of Georgie's palm.

She dares not look down because a tree is rising beside her now, full and dense, a living, breathing tree. Her fingertips reach to touch and, even as this happens, she feels a sharp yank on her body. As she is being pulled towards an opening of light, she hears an explosion of laughter, her own.

"I could become the tree," she says and, improbably, she laughs again. Once more, she extends her fingertips, this time to feel the roughness of bark. Tendons are taut along her wrists and hands. Her car is nowhere to be seen. Why is she separate from

7

her car? Something orange, a clot in the eye, rolls past and drops out of sight. But Georgie is still moving. And now, for reasons she cannot explain, she is stretched out on her back. Roots grow savagely from the earth and slam her ribs. Her scapula is stabbed by a lightning edge of rock. Root or rock, her flight has ended. Georgie has sunk to the bottom of Spinney's Ravine.

TWO

Is the hip broken? The leg? Which? She understands that
the pain is so great, her body is not large enough to hold it.
It leaps from her forehead, her nose, her joints, her mouth;
it oozes from a gash in the side of her neck; it wraps up her
heels and ribs; it thrusts a javelin into her cheekbone and
heaves a sword, which splits her thigh. It hovers above the lids
of her eyes and sinks deep into her orbits. She stares straight
up and is surprised to see the forked branch of a tree, a pad-
ding of cloud that tucks up the edges of sky. On the ground,
lumps of darkness threaten and spread around her. Words
cartwheel across her mind and she squints, hard, in an effort
to slow them down: *wheel pillow palace tree wheel pillow palace tree.* No other sound is contained in memory, no matter
how much she pries.

THREE

Is she dead?

"Harry!" she calls. "Am I dead?"

She has to move. Of course she has to move. After a certain age, the body must be kept moving or the bones will seize. Where is she? She hasn't done her walk today: half-mile down the hill, half-mile up. She's walked the hill so many years, she can do it in her sleep. Twice a week, and she misses occasionally, but the walk has kept her fit. She can do it in winter in her Bama Lams; she can do it in spring and summer and fall.

She's cold. Shaking. She's been unconscious—or was it only sleep? She has seen the most unusual tree. She is on her way somewhere. But where?

The queen did not like him, nor did the king
So Hector Protector was sent home again

Sequential disarray. She remembers those two words. What do they mean? She's somewhere, lining up her thoughts. Flat on her back, but she's not sure where. Most certainly not in her bed.

Concentrate. Think of the bones, she tells herself. *Are there any broken bones?*

The ones she can't move.

Try the left leg.

It bends.

Try the right.

Pain, shooting through.

Fingers?

Fine.

Left arm?

It's fine, too.

Right arm?

She's afraid to lift. Her shoulder might be crushed.

Spine?

She can wiggle her toes. She wouldn't be able to if her spine . . .

She must not be morbid. She thinks of Hubley the skeleton, rattling off the page of her grandfather's anatomy book, the one she discovered at the country house the year she started school. At one time, she could rhyme off every one of Hubley's bones.

Cranium: occipital, frontal, parietal. She's missing some. Slowly now. Temporal, maxillary, mandible.

Vomer, shaped like a ploughshare. A fossil of memory jumps to her consciousness like an old secret revealed.

Atlas.

Axis. The pivot that allows her to turn her head.

She raises her head the tiniest bit. Turns it a little, tips it to the right and back. Sees bushes, trees; a feather, snagged by a burr of rock; a curved rib, rubbed grey—not human. And there, in a clearing behind her, the length of a room away, is the car, bashed and battered, the driver's door sprung. How can the car be upright when it flipped and somersaulted all the way down? It hit branches, a tree; she was inside, she should know. There isn't much to remember. How then? She's been thrown clear. The door is wide open. Was she not wearing her belt?

She was not.

Not this time.

So, it's her own fault.

She could bend one knee, push with one foot, attempt to get to the car, inch by inch on her back, reach up inside, honk the horn. But her head is resting on a thin ridge of rock. The only way to relieve the pain is to raise her head, let it loll, bang it down. And the pain starts all over again.

What would the Queen do?

The Queen would not have been behind the wheel. She'd have had a chauffeur.

She was on her way to the palace. Her face has been slammed. Her mouth is dry and cold as ash. She might go into shock. *The first principle of healing is rest.* She learned that from Grandfather's medical books. Why did Harry have to buy a black car? No one will see it down here when dusk falls. Only a moment ago, it was morning. She saw Case in daylight, and that was afternoon. Someone lifted something orange into the car. Her daughter. Case.

She said her farewells.

But who is she?

She wonders if someone like her has been given a name.

She sleeps.

FOUR

I f someone would just say how long she's been here, she'd be grateful. Three hours or thirteen. One day or two.

Surely not two.

She has to think of night. The number of times it's been dark. One. She saw darkness. No, she dreamed the dark. She must have been unconscious. Otherwise, she'd have been frightened. She's frightened now. If only she could stop shivering.

She stares into an upturned root that has been wrenched up and off the ground, but is still attached to the base of a giant tree. The root, longer than her body, arcs like a crocodile that had its belly slit mid-air. It's even complete with a cold, dark eye. The tree must be half-alive, half-dead; it lists heavily and there are no branches on one side. Her eyes follow the lean all the way to slanted sky. She's forced to squint because it pains her to look at the waning light. Does she have a bruised orbit? Is one eye swollen? Thirst scrapes at her throat like a claw. She sees a motley patch of cloud attached to a long stem. As it trembles, her bones sway with its motion. A crow caws, out of sight, and then barks like a sick dog.

Who has not imagined horror? She wants to howl, but what good will howling do? If she closes her eyes, darkness will fall. It behooves her to think of morning light.

The word *behooves* drops into her mind like a discarded password rediscovered. The word *behooves* makes her want to weep. She raises her head and once more looks back towards the car. At the same moment, she clearly and accurately remembers her own name.

FEMUR

FIVE

My family calls me George, sometimes Georgie, but my full name is Georgina Danforth Witley. I am familiar with pain, the kind of knowledge that comes with age.

Am I dead?

Harry?

Don't answer. If you do, I'll *know* I'm dead.

My left hand rests in soot. When I pat the earth, I come up with a piece of charred bark. Did someone build a fire on this very spot? My coat will be dirty.

Soot is not a priority. Not here.

Who are you? The silent inquisitor?

You're practically home. Your two-storey house is up the hill, the driveway bare, the front door locked. It's out of sight, but you know it's there.

The door wants painting. It's begun to chip. My ivies will need watering. I was on my way.

The ivies are hardy. They'll survive. The woods are the same that grow outside your back stoop; the treed hill descends.

I'm in the ravine, then. I'm at the bottom of Spinney's Ravine.

This is an outrage. I'll miss my appointment with the Queen. Surely not. I'll get up. All I have to do is move.

SIX

I must save myself or be rescued. It is that clear. But why would anyone search? I'm not missing. It was my decision to go alone. Phil is probably sitting in the lounge at the Haven this very moment, thinking I'm walking the streets of London. Or maybe she thinks I'm still on the plane. Has an hour passed? A day?

My hips don't lie right. There is rock beneath my body no matter which way I squirm. The femur feels as if it has snapped. If it did fracture, the break is high up. I don't think it's my hip. Surely not my hip, that old cliché.

If Case were here, she'd tilt that head of coal-black hair she inherited from the Danforth gene pool and she'd look directly into me and say, *You're in shock, Mother. Lie still and don't panic.*

Yes, Case would take charge. She's used to giving directions; it's her nature. She doesn't know what she sounds like, it's just the way she is. So thoroughly does she believe she's in charge, it makes me love her all the more.

But I haven't panicked. Not yet. Someone will come. I just have to wait. Still, I wish Case were here.

Casey Brown
Went downtown
With her trousers
Hanging down

The children taunted on her first day of school. She was six years old and her underpants had a serious droop. Didn't matter, because she knew how to laugh. "My name's not Brown!" she challenged, ignoring the matter of the underwear. The taunt did not get her down. When you laugh at your tormentors, you disarm them. She knew that, even then.

My heart is racing; my bones have collapsed. There is the matter of the femur, but if I can move myself in bits, I might get closer to the car. As long as I don't make things worse. I have one good arm, don't I? I can use it to straighten the other. My disabled limbs seem not to belong to me. But I can push with one heel. I can bunch a fistful of pant leg with my good hand, drag the bad leg, the one that's been so quick to disown me.

I'll do what has to be done.

There must be wide spaces between posts up there. Strange that I've never noticed. If the car had hit a railing, it might have been deflected. But no, it had to find an open spot. The sense of error, of loss, was immediate. I remember that. But it's my road, the one I've navigated thousands of times. I live up there. It's where my bed is. Where my body wants to be. Harry and I chose the house because of the attraction of living above the ravine. We loved the place when we first saw it.

Harry touched his finger to the door and made an *X*, moments before we made our offer. "It's ours," he said. "Can't you feel that it's ours?" And I could. It was where we belonged. The front windows looked down over the town; the back, over the edge of the ravine. There was a large backyard, a cul-de-sac at the end of the street. And ours was the first of only four houses at the top of the hill.

My car is not in the driveway; someone will notice and report my absence. But my neighbours know I was on my way to London. The whole town read about the Queen's invitation in the *Wilna Creek Times*. They used a photograph I don't like. It was taken from the side and I was caught off guard, no time to raise my chin. It made me look older than I am; it made me look crabby.

Here's a crow, cawing high above.

Hello! Hello! Is anyone there?

I refuse to stay here, but how can I get up? The tiniest movement is beyond me.

That's defeat talking.

Well, I hurt. That isn't defeat. What I need is a blanket to pull over my head. It would make me feel better.

At least I remember who I am.

Then start moving, Georgie. Get yourself started.

I will, after I rest. I need a moment, just a moment, to rest.

SEVEN

God? Are You here? Are You near?

I dreamed I was floating upwards, but I have plummeted all the way down. No one will see the car. Harry chose black because he thought it looked expensive. Pride, one of the deadly sins, though I don't mean to tattle. He died the year after the purchase, his death unrelated—You would know.

Am I meant to die in the ravine? Is this a long-range plan? If so, why did You spare me on the way down? The lack of warning is truly frightening.

I haven't been in touch for a while, I know. Last time I was at morning service, I had a coughing fit and had to remove myself to a rear pew. I left before the service was over and haven't been back. Phil attends chapel at the Haven on Sundays and I don't have to pick her up any more. Truth to tell, I haven't made the effort to go by myself.

There should be tire marks on the shoulder up there. The miracle is, my shell is cracked but I don't feel so damaged inside.

I must be scratched, bruised, splattered with blood, though it's hard to see.

Stay on track, Georgie. You were talking to God. Perhaps prayer will help. Any prayer will do. Try to remember the Creed.

It's been a while. I'll stare at the sky and concentrate. There's nothing up there but an underbelly of cloud that blocks most of the light. Or is darkness descending?

Go ahead, try the prayer.

I believe in God, the Father Almighty
Maker of heaven and earth

When you first look at a thing, sometimes you don't see it clearly. A ragged rock, longer than my humerus, is trapped deep inside the decay of the giant root. And there are smooth stones, palm-sized, tucked as if they've been pocketed. The root must have set its trap when alive and underground. How slowly it would have grown around those cool, hard stones. And then— to lift them up as part of itself and break through earth.

Ibelieveingodthefatheralmightymakerofheavenandearthand injesuschristhisonlysonour

Brain is tired, head won't work. When I was a child, I couldn't understand why an entire congregation of Anglicans faced front and declared themselves to believe in the Catholic Church. There was a *k* at the end of the word in my parents' prayer book—*Catholick*.

The Holy Catholick Church
The Communion of Sins—surely that should be Saints
The Communion of Saints

I'm rusty. I've forgotten the words. Ribs and bum are stuck to Canadian Shield. The woods around have begun to moan and breathe—or is it my own moaning and breathing I hear?

Nicene! Another version. Yanked from a fold of grey matter, the word bobs like a float in the mind. My grandmother, Grand Dan, said I had the memory of an unwiped slate. But memory can also be a curse.

Perhaps God will send someone to look for me in this abyss.

Not very likely in these darkening shadows.

Ah, the night drops over me, like a hood.

EIGHT

Morning light touches my hair and reminds that I'm alive. When I tilt my head, the same ray of sunshine strikes my forehead—so warm, I want to cry out in gratitude. I have one useless arm, one useless leg. And what good is the rest of me, attached to both?

Wings above. The crow again, a solo crow.

It's me, Georgie! Send someone down! I'm at the bottom of the ravine.

What if no one's looking? Shouldn't you be moving?

I think I've moved a little. Anyway, someone has to start looking. Case will be driving up the hill to bring in mail, check the house. But when? How often? Not every day. She'll drive past the railings and see shrubs flattened, signs of violence or surprise. Or will she bother to look to the side? She's always in a hurry.

I can't solve all of these problems at once. I don't even know what day it is. I received an invitation from the palace. The Queen and I were born the same day.

You have a watch, Georgie. Check the date on it.

I can set the hour and the minute but I've never figured out how to set the date. Harry bought the watch in Geneva, when we were on our Big Trip. He was a jeweller himself, and wanted me to pay attention when his Swiss counterpart adjusted the settings. I confess that I ignored the instructions. My only interest was in having a watch with a face large enough to see.

Our interests diverged, Harry's and mine. Out of his entire record collection, Teresa Brewer was his favourite. While Django Reinhardt was the man for me. Anyone would think the match was doomed, but we managed in other, loving ways. As for Django, I have Case's partner, Rice, to thank for that. Rice plays jazz guitar, and came up the hill bearing gifts of old music. Ever since, Django has kept me company.

You're getting sidetracked, Georgie. Look at the watch.

All right then. My glasses must be somewhere. In my purse, or cracked and broken. I don't wear them for driving.

What was I thinking when the car sailed over the edge?

My watch will break.

Surely not something so banal. That could have been my last thought. One hopes for something grander. Still, the watch means something. It was a gift from Harry. I can make out the arrows, but they're not moving.

Time seems kind of pointless, down here.

Put on your glasses.

They wouldn't help. In any case, they're missing.

What do you mean, missing?

I mean I'm tired. I'm running out of thoughts.

You! Running out of thoughts.

Shouldn't I be trying to move?

Remember Grandfather's first principle.

The first principle of healing is rest. That was easy.

Memory floats in, memory floats out. You don't have to move the whole distance at once.

What distance? How far? I was certain I was floating when I fell. I saw transparent leaves, the glass tree. It was given to my grandfather and, years after his death, passed on to me. Grand Dan wanted me to have it. I heard glass breaking; fragments scattered over the floor.

You're shivering, Georgie. You're cold. Gather your coat around you. Keep calm.

My coat is unbuttoned, though I'm wearing my cardigan beneath. I'm supposed to find pigskin gloves in London for my mother. I drove to the Haven to say goodbye, and asked what she wanted me to bring back. She was sitting small on the seat of her walker, shoulders seriously humped. When did Phil last have her bone density checked? I towered over her, though we've both shrunk. She raised her head and said, "Bring me pigskin gloves."

"When will you wear pigskin gloves in here?"

She clucked her tongue as if she'd brought me into the world only to discover, almost eighty years later, that I'm useless. "You asked what I wanted."

"What colour, then?"

"Piggy colour, what else?"

Oh, Mother. I loved her at that moment, but what a motherlode is she. She's a true mistress of evasion, but she never gives up. She's the only resident of the Haven who is over a hundred, and describes herself as "Edwardian—just." I'm convinced that she has managed to live so long because she's thin and wiry and moves her body easily. She holds on to her walker because it helps her balance, but she can move without it, too. And she's small. She inherited the short genes of the family, and I the tall.

She's also a lurker, capable of moving into minds. She's been hovering at the edge of my mind every day of my life and here I am in my eighth decade and I am still someone's child. Maybe that's the way it is with mothers and daughters. Maybe she lurks in my sister's mind, too. Ally lives so far away, she's probably immune. I'll phone and ask her sometime, after I've been rescued.

If I'm rescued.

Don't think bad thoughts, Georgie. You're alive.

True enough. But I've missed my chance to break bread with the Queen. I'll be the only one not to show. Will the Master of the Household discreetly remove my fork, my silver goblet, my chair?

Sometimes I talk to Elizabeth, though she's never heard my conversations. The fact that my life and hers were following a pattern early on did not escape my notice, and I began to think fondly of her as Lilibet, a kind of parallel life-mate. Once, I even saw her up close—not so many years ago. She was visiting Canada and on her way to open a new agricultural college in the next town. Her limo was driven all the way from Ottawa with a police escort and had to pass through Wilna Creek, through the intersection of Ross and Main. A policeman stood in front of pedestrians at the corner, intending to hold us back. When I saw the limo approach, I peered around the uniformed shoulder, and there she was. She waved directly at me from the back seat as if we were old friends, as if she had heard me talking to her all these years. She wore a bemused look on her face: *Look where we find ourselves today.*

Well, look where I find myself today. Mouth dry, lips that

feel like parched earth cracking. Is this the day of Lilibet's celebration? And who refuses the Queen? I'd gladly march to the palace if only someone would help me to get up.

I'm not from a family of whiners. I shall be steadfast—a word Grand Dan loved. I need a solid plan that does not allow an inch of room for feeling sorry for myself.

But thoughts creep from their shelter, welcome or not. My family riffles like cards through my head. My history peers back at me. Who is dead? Who is not? With a mother as old as mine, you want to know your stories. The endings, I'm not so sure of. People die holding their secrets, their loves, their pains. History is rewritten. I know that Case hasn't taken the time yet to hear the stories, but maybe someday she'll want to know about the family that came before her.

Who, for instance, would have predicted that I would end up sandwiched between a daughter in her fifties and a mother who is a hundred and three? Each has a free side to do as she pleases, but I am in the middle, tucked to both like cheese on rye. Case decided to love a jazz musician. Phil loved my father, who owned the dry goods store in town. I chose to love Harry, a jeweller. Phil and Case and I may be from different generations, but we still share the same unbroken line of the past.

NINE

And so I am stuck, a beetle on my back, talking to myself. I am the daughter of Philomena Danforth and the late Conrad Holmes, Conrad with a *C*. My father died after a long illness in 1945, shortly after my sister Ally's wedding. His store was on Main Street in Wilna Creek, and everyone in town called him Mr. Holmes, even family. We all helped out in the store at one time or another, and frequently heard ourselves saying, "Let me ask Mr. Holmes about that. I'll check with Mr. Holmes." He died so long ago I have to strain to hear his shouts—and he did shout. At least that's what I remember. He also wore a black patch, having been blinded by a stick in one eye as a child. I never met another member of his family, nor did my mother. His family was from the *old country*, he once said, and I saw his one eye water as he turned away. To me, the *old country* meant something vague, like the north of England, maybe a coal town in Wales. He had been an only child, and his parents were dead long before Ally and I were born. In some ways, Mr. Holmes was a mystery man in town.

The women of the family took it for granted that they would outlive their men. It's the way life keeps turning out. I've outlived Harry. Grand Dan outlived my grandfather, a doctor who was killed in the First Great War. Phil has outlived my father by more than sixty years, though she alarms people because she can faint at will. She drops to the floor when it pleases her, even at the Haven, though she's careful how she falls. The Queen Mother outlived her husband; Victoria outlived Albert; Queen Mary outlived George V. It's the way things have always been.

I am from a family of ones: one mother, one father, one sister, one niece, one aunt, one uncle, one grandmother, one husband, one child, alive, Cassandra. We've always called her Case and, from the beginning, she loved her name.

Harry, too, was an only—at least we thought he was. He was born in England, and came to the marriage alone.

Grand Dan was a midwife. The last baby she officially delivered was me, on April 21, 1926. Regulations were changing; provincial laws were put in place. She delivered a few babies after me, but only when a doctor couldn't be reached. When I came along, I knew from the time I could talk that Princess Elizabeth of York and I had entered the world on the same day. My sister Ally had already been born, two years before me. All our lives, we've counted on each other: Ally and George, Georgie and Al.

There! I've managed to drag the bad leg behind me, but only three or four inches. Without painkillers. For all the progress I've made, I could have spared myself the discomfort. I won't say the pain is unbearable, because I have no choice; I have to bear it.

I've borne worse.

Say it out, then, Georgie.

Death. Darkness. I've had dark days. I try not to retreat into old shadows, but they're there. I know they're there.

Life apportions, life takes away.

I must not take on dark thoughts. If I get to the car, I might find something useful. Bandages. The first-aid kit has never been lifted out of the trunk. Even if I could reach it, what would I bandage and how, with one hand? My right arm won't move. Good arm, bad arm. Good leg, bad leg. My knee hurts but at least it creaks and bends. I feel the extraordinary weight of myself, heavier than I know my body to be. It's the sensation I have after a bath if I stay in the tub while the water is running out.

It would be more of a worry, Georgie, if you couldn't feel your body at all.

That is the truth.

The car doesn't seem so far now, though it's not easy to judge. I feel as if I'm upside down. My thoughts are scattered, like the glass leaves.

I'll try to remember what was in the car, front and back. My purse. Case's gift, orange paper stuffed into the bag. I saw it drop somewhere as I flew past. My suitcase, in the trunk. Everything rearranged.

I'm rearranged. I must order my thoughts. Right my body. If the mind can right itself, so can the body. I'll try to imagine myself sitting, standing. But not climbing the side of the ravine. I can't do that.

Can't?

Didn't I tell Case when she was a child, her small round face looking up at me, "Never say can't"?

Who said that?

Every one of the women in my family for four generations, that's who.

TIBIA

TEN

I must keep my brain talking. Perhaps I tried the wrong prayer. The Creed was never relaxed, to my way of thinking. Not like the Lord's Prayer.

Prayers of my childhood. The sturdiness of Ontario stone. Our solid country church on the Wilna Creek Road. Ally took my hand as we followed Grand Dan, Phil and Mr. Holmes up the aisle every Sunday, our own small footsteps echoing theirs. We slid across the third-row pew on the right, the same in which Danforths had been accountable to God for generations. Grand Dan presided, and cast an eye back over the narrow room before she kneeled to pray. She had smacked the bare bottoms of more than half the congregation, and had forced their first intake of breath. I suppose she considered all of us her children—we who had been delivered into her long fingers, we who had been anointed with olive oil poured to a saucer by her caring midwife's hands.

We stood for the Apostles' Creed and I waited for the part where everyone bobbed heads at the same instant. Between half-closed lids, I caught rows of nods out of the corner of my eye. Grand Dan, high above me—long and thin in a plain grey coat that hung to her ankles—looked down with a different head movement, one I well understood, to let me know I was not to stare. I was expected to join in, and I did my best, speeding the lines, trying not to think of the countless bums Grand Dan had smacked and what the congregation would look like if they suddenly dropped their drawers and bared them.

We had to kneel for the Lord's Prayer, and we flipped the kneeling board towards us on its hinges. At the end of the service, we flipped it back. I liked the mechanics of the kneeling board, the collaboration of sharers of the pew. It was about silent co-operation, timing, eye and hand signals. The board yielded; it was out of sight. As it disappeared, I rolled my eyes skyward and whispered for my dead grandfather's benefit, *Structure determines function*, thinking how pleased he must have been when he had sat in the same pew. That was the second of his principles, his three grand thoughts, the ones I found written in his handwriting on the inside cover of *Anatomy, Descriptive and Surgical* by Henry Gray.

During my childhood, it was my stinging regret that I did not have the opportunity to meet my grandfather, Dr. Matthias Danforth, who was born in Wilna Creek but went away to Toronto to be educated as a physician. He returned in 1900 at the start of a promising new century, and married the woman he loved, the midwife with the long black hair and the no-nonsense reputation, the woman who had waited for him while he completed his education. He began to work at the newly constructed three-storey hospital in the growing town of Wilna Creek. The roads were no longer made of planks, and cedar boardwalks were gradually being replaced. His parents were dead and he and his black-haired bride moved two country miles to the Danforth family home, which he had inherited. They were the same age when they married, twenty-five. Grand Dan—affectionately called "Danny" by my grandfather after their marriage—had one known indulgence, a love of gardening and, in particular, of yellow roses.

Grandfather travelled back and forth to town by horse and buggy for years and finally purchased his first automobile in 1913. It was Brewster green, a Model T nicknamed "the Rooster." At the white house in the country, he turned the Danforth library into a consulting room for patients who insisted on showing up at his back door, expected or not. He installed a leather-topped examining table and a panelled screen behind which patients could disrobe. With hospital work in town, house calls and home office in the country, he must have had dreams of being a gentleman farmer as well as a professional man. But only two years after he bought the Rooster, he opened the double doors of the sagging shed, drove the Model T inside, asked Grand Dan to give it a polish now and then and marched off to war. He was older than most of his medical colleagues, older than all of the soldiers he cared for, but determined to do his duty. Casualty lists had filtered back and he could not abide the thought of young boys of nineteen or twenty needing amputations, bleeding to death in dressing stations before there was time to carry them back behind the lines. He had the skills, and wanted them tested under conditions that were extreme.

He left by train from Wilna Creek Station with the hospital staff waving him off. At the time of his departure in 1915, he and Grand Dan were forty years old. They had two daughters: my mother, Philomena, called Phil, and her sister, Freda, known to everyone as Fred.

After that, there is a gap in the story between 1915 and 1916. Letters must have been exchanged during that time but I have never seen them, though I've longed to. Grand Dan was private and, before she died, she must have destroyed every trace of her lost love.

This is what I was told by my mother. In France in the fall of 1916, a soldier from our little town suffered a terrible leg injury at the Somme. By chance, he was helped to an Advance Dressing Station in which my grandfather was senior Medical Officer in charge. After being treated by my grandfather—who was well acquainted with the young man and greeted him as a father would a son—the soldier was lifted onto a stretcher. He was in pain but alert, and promised that if he made it home from Blighty, he would go to visit the doctor's wife. Wanting to prolong the encounter, my grandfather stepped outside the Dressing Station and, just after the stretcher-bearers started back towards the rear, a shell exploded near the entrance to the hut that he was about to re-enter. The soldier lived to tell the tale and eventually returned to Canada with an artificial limb. My grandfather was blown to bits.

In 1917, exactly one year after the date of his injury, on the anniversary of my grandfather's death, the limping soldier arrived at the house to tell Grand Dan about her husband's last moments and the three sentences he had uttered before the fatal shellburst. "If I don't make it back, tell my Danny she'll always be the love of my life. Tell her I had no choice. I had to do what I could."

Grand Dan stood at the door and listened intently to the words the soldier had committed to memory and kept inside him for a full year. "The doctor must have had a premonition," he added sadly. "It happened over there, all the time."

Grand Dan received the message with dignity, committed the words to her own memory and brought the soldier into the house to offer him a cup of tea and a slice of War cake, which she had made earlier that morning. Having no oil for cooking, she had stirred bacon grease into the cake, hoping that ginger and cloves would overpower the taste of bacon. She did not cry. She had already been silenced the previous year, the day the news of her husband's death was delivered by telegram.

That story, about the telegram of the year before, 1916, is the one that accounts for Grand Dan wrapping her legs. And wrap them she did, every day until she died. Aunt Fred passed the story on to me, when I was a child.

When the telegram came, Aunt Fred was eleven years old and in school, as was my then thirteen-year-old mother. No one was at the house except Grand Dan herself, and the deliverer of the telegram, Brainy Knapp.

Aunt Fred, who had hay fever all her life, told the story in her stuffed-up, nasal voice. She had managed to marry a man also called Fred, so the two were known to Ally and me as Aunt and Uncle Fred. My uncle used to say, "My Freddie has enough twang to make a fortune as a country-and-western singer," and this infuriated my aunt. Still, I thought it could be true. Aunt and Uncle Fred fought throughout their entire marriage, but they were passionately in love. They argued over whether the window sash should be up or down, who left scum on the bar of Lifebuoy soap and whether the cream that popped out of the top of the milk bottle in winter should be spooned off or stirred. "We're sticking it out for the long haul," Aunt Fred said, as if to ward off family criticism. But no one criticized, and I, for one, did not doubt their love.

This is how Aunt Fred told the story. Brainy Knapp, whom

Grand Dan had tugged into the world feet first from between his mother's thighs, rode his bicycle out from town, turned into the lane and found the doctor's wife close to the stoop in the backyard, splitting kindling with an axe. When she saw him dismount his bicycle and head towards her, she foresaw the news before he had a chance to hand over the telegram. Because she was distracted, she swung the blade of the axe hard against her own right leg and chopped the skin over the bone, the tibia, for which I always had a melancholy fondness after hearing the story.

Grand Dan did not scream when she axed her tibia. It was Brainy who filled the air with blood-curdling shrieks. Grand Dan ordered Brainy into the house to fetch a long linen towel from the kitchen roller. He dropped the telegram, which she picked up off the ground when he ran to the house. The paper was soaked in blood before she unfolded it. Because her daughters were at school, there was no one to help but Brainy. By the time he pulled the towel off the roller and ran outside again, Grand Dan had dragged herself from the stoop to the kitchen door, leaving a trail of flattened grass and spurted blood. She wrapped her own leg to stop the bleeding, and commanded Brainy to tuck his head between his knees and take deep breaths so he wouldn't pass out. He was inconsolable over the impact of the doctor's death, combined with my grandmother's accident, which he believed he had caused by being the bearer of bad news. The telegram was carried inside.

Grand Dan bore no ill will towards the messenger, but from that day forward she remained silent about my grandfather's death. The tibia was another matter. It was slow to heal because chronic osteomyelitis had set in, and she applied herbal compresses for months before she was able to stop the wound from oozing. She did not go to town to have her injury looked after by her husband's colleagues. Instead, when the oozing ceased, she wrapped not one but both legs with rolls of bandage, which she made by tearing strips of white cotton, two and a half inches wide. She called the bandages her "cottons," and wrapped them around her legs every day of her life.

Fifteen years after the telegram—by this time Ally and I had been born and our family had moved to Grand Dan's house in the country—I finally saw her legs without the cottons. Grand Dan and I were first up every morning, and she tolerated my stares as I watched her do the encircling wraps before the rest of the family came down for breakfast. One leg at a time, she anchored the bandage around the sole of her foot, twined it about the ankle and circled it upwards until it reached the knee. Over the bandages, she pulled tan-coloured lisle stockings. She slid her wedding garters, one at a time, up over her thighs, and rolled the tops of the stockings back down over the garters, which disappeared under her dress.

I was the one who saw the mottled patches of brown that had begun to cover both legs, which were exposed to light only momentarily at the beginning of each day. One morning, I was brave enough to look her in the eye and say, "May I touch your telegram scar, Grand Dan?" She gave me a long look and then leaned back and said, "You may." I ran two fingers over the hardened scar left by the axe, and it did not disappoint. It was as if a twisted vein had slipped out of her leg and calcified, and fastened itself lengthwise to the outside of her shin. No diagram in my grandfather's medical books could match it. I did not mention being allowed to touch the scar to my sister, though it did occur to me that Ally might not be jealous, since she had interests of her own.

Once the stockings were in place, the surface of Grand Dan's legs was smooth and disguised. There wasn't a wrinkle or fold between one layer of bandage and the next. Nor could an inch of skin be seen between the hem of her dress and her feet, which disappeared into black lace-up shoes. Every second day, she washed her cottons with Fels-Naptha, creating suds with the wire soap-saver that was tied by a string to the backboard behind the sink. She hung the strips on the line to dry and, when I came home from school, it was my job to go outside to fetch them. In winter they froze on the line and, after I unpegged them, I carried them over my shoulder like swords and brought them in and propped their stiff forms against the wall. At a single moment, they thawed, crinkled and collapsed to the floor without warning.

Grand Dan wound her hair into a bun every morning, and kept it there with the longest hairpins she could buy. She wore a fringed, black shawl around her shoulders, even in summer. It was left to me in her will and though I still have it, it is worn to tatters. I can't bring myself to throw it away, or cut it up for dusters.

I could use Grand Dan's shawl right now. I've begun to get a chill from the ground beneath me. My coat helps; my cardigan helps—it's made of tightly knit boiled wool. I bought it in the Austrian Tyrol when Harry and I were on our trip. The only problem is, it's green, like my coat, which means I don't have much hope of being detected. Especially with the branches above me straining to burst into leaf. The landscape could wrap itself around me and I'd never be seen.

And now, a blast of sun warms my cheek. A blessing from Sol. As Aunt Fred used to say, "It's enough to make you weep."

But you won't weep, Georgie. What good would that do? Do

something to save yourself. Keep moving. Get into the open. Suck the buttons on the cardigan.

I read somewhere that sucking buttons creates saliva. If you have no water, if you are in dire straits.

You are in dire straits. Look around you. See where you are.

I'm thirsty. My mouth is dry. The cardigan has silver buttons with an imprint of a crown. Buttons of royalty. Lilibet might have such a sweater. I can reach the top three, maybe four, with my left hand, pull them up to my chin. Bottom ones, too, though it makes no difference; it isn't as if buttons have flavours. I haven't thought about food; it's water I want. The tiniest bit could save me. A bit of saliva might fool the thirst.

Structure determines function. Suck the buttons. You'll be saved. Don't get yourself worked up.

I'm not getting worked up. What good would that do? But I'm restless. Clots might be forming in my veins. Clots can kill. I need to raise my leg, the good one. The other is a burning poker. If only I could see what damage lies beneath my pant leg. If Ally were with me, we'd laugh. One recess, while we played outside our one-room school, we were told by an older boy that his parents had a book called "Lifter Leg and Poker." "Ha Ha," the children around us shouted, "Ha Ha." We thought this hilarious, but didn't know what it meant. We giggled insanely until we said it aloud in Grand Dan's kitchen, and were promptly sent to our room.

Grand Dan's house, Grand Dan's rules. That was 1932, shortly after Phil and Mr. Holmes moved us two miles out of the town of Wilna Creek and into Phil's childhood home, the Danforth house. From that day forward, Ally and I had three adults to obey instead of two.

ELEVEN

The reason my parents moved our family was because Grand Dan had decided she no longer wanted to live alone—seventeen years since my grandfather had left for war was seventeen years too many—so we obliged her by moving in. We were closest; therefore, Grand Dan was our responsibility. I was six years old and Ally was eight.

Our Aunt and Uncle Fred lived a hundred and sixty miles west along what was known as the King's Highway. Uncle Fred, who had been born in Austria-Hungary before the Great War, emigrated from the new Austria when he was fifteen. He always told us he had a charmed life: too young to fight in the Great War, he'd survived the upheaval afterwards. He ended up in our little Ontario town, wooed my Aunt Fred, and then followed a railroad job after they married. Enough years had passed that it was deemed inconvenient for them to move back to Wilna Creek to help out. They were part of their own community now; they were raising four sons. Uncle Fred had become an inspector and wore a white shirt to work.

Ally and I loved our Uncle Fred. He was a storyteller, a bawdy-joke man, a believer in ghosts. But we also knew that when his sons misbehaved, he held their heads under the outdoor pump. I saw him do this to the eldest when I was visiting their family one summer. He pumped until a great sucking sound pulled a sob out of the earth, and cold water gushed over my cousin's neck. Because of this and even though I loved him, I was glad Uncle Fred was not our father. We had our own set of problems with Mr. Holmes. *Our* father was a ranter and a shouter—but only at night, in his sleep.

No one thought it strange that our grandmother did not move to town to live with us. I suppose our parents thought she had lost enough. She should not be required to lose husband *and* home in one lifetime.

Grand Dan's house in the country was not huge but had a high-ceilinged library, an enclosed veranda, a small parlour, large kitchen with a windowed pantry, and summer kitchen, which was closed off in winter. Upstairs, there were three bedrooms with slanted ceilings. Ally and I shared a room and slept together in a big double bed. The house whispered and breathed like bellows. It had the scent of stored apples, the sound of ancestral spirits walking corridors and rapping walls. Downstairs, in the parlour, there was a huge floor-model radio that had walnut latticework across its front, as well as an extra dial for short-wave. Ally and I listened to dots and dashes, imagined ships stranded at sea.

Apart from the house, Grand Dan owned a large field, leased as a hayfield to Mott, a neighbouring farmer who raised cows and pigs. The wide shed into which Grandfather had driven his Model T had a severe tilt. The car had aged but was still running and, for a few years, our father drove it back and forth to the dry goods store in town. He sold the car—with Grand Dan's approval—and bought another, second-hand, after learning that the barber on Main Street had been overheard to say, one morning, "Here comes one-eyed Holmes in his flivver."

There was another outbuilding on the country property, a small chicken coop, and for a time, Grand Dan raised hens and chicks. One of the few photos taken at the time shows Mott standing beside Grand Dan and holding two plucked, upside-down hens, their necks wrung. Grand Dan was wearing a bloody white apron—she made her aprons from flour bags—though Mott would have been called to do the neck-wringing. Our grandmother could not bring herself to end a life, even though she had to cook the hens to feed the family.

Twice a week, Wednesday and Saturday, Mott delivered milk and cream in graniteware cans to our back door, part of the bargain concerning the lease of the field. In 1937, he purchased a narrow strip of that same field. He would have bought more, but Grand Dan kept the larger portion against needier times. For the moment, the sale provided enough cash to stretch out over a few more years. She was cordial at the time of the sale, but never fully approved of Mott because he'd once lit a fire under his horse, Dandy, who'd balked and refused to move.

Outside, Grand Dan planted yellow roses inside the spokes of an enormous wagon wheel that had been rolled to the backyard and laid on its side over rocky soil, which she had nurtured and fertilized since the turn of the century. The rest of the yard was a vegetable garden that reached as far as the low stone wall. Grand Dan had been a June baby, and every year on her birthday the first yellow rose bloomed. How these events managed to coincide was a mystery to Ally and me.

Grandfather had left little money in the bank, but there was a small pension, and the house was free of mortgage. After our family moved in, the women worked to keep the place up. My father occupied himself with the store in town and, until sales began to falter badly during the last years of the Great Depression, the five of us had enough to live on.

Not only did Grandfather leave a Model T, a wife and two daughters behind, he also left his medical books. The day we moved to the country house, I discovered them in the Danforth library, exactly as they had been abandoned. Grand Dan had kept the room more or less intact, except for a sewing table, which took up the centre. A pedal-operated Singer was squeezed against one wall and challenged the examining table for space. Shelved along another wall were medical texts and the remainder of Grandfather's library: Dickens in fifteen volumes, Count Leo Tolstoy, *The Poems of Archibald Lampman*, six volumes of Conan Doyle, *The Deerslayer* by James Fenimore Cooper, *Uncle Tom's Cabin* by H. B. Stowe. Presiding over the entire room was a framed portrait of Queen Victoria, a sideways view.

My fascination with human anatomy began the day I let myself into this room and shut the door behind me. I scanned the shelves, lifted down the thickest book, plopped it on the sun-warmed leather of the examining table and opened the cover to inspect the diagrams. I was six years old, and that was the day my obsession with learning truly began. As it turned out, my favourite of all the books was *Gray's Anatomy*, 1901, the one I returned to most frequently and the first I had pulled from the shelf. You might say a kind of imprinting took place. It was also there that I encountered Grandfather's cramped handwriting, words written in tight squiggles on the inside cover. I did my best to decipher his writings—he had also jotted in the margins—and throughout my childhood, I pondered what I considered to be his three grand thoughts.

The first principle of healing is rest.

Structure determines function.

The third must have been written at a later time; it was in a slightly different hand and a darker ink.

Learning is changed behaviour.

This was still my grandfather's handwriting, but the writing had become expansive and hurried. I suppose he had a lot on his mind. Or maybe he'd learned to change his behaviour. Young as I was, I recognized that the three grand thoughts were direct messages from him to me, messages that partially satisfied my prying mind.

For years, the text portion was gibberish to me, even though I knew how to read in rudimentary fashion. Ally, who had started school before me, had taught me most of what she had learned. But what most captivated me about *Gray's* were the illustrations. I was fascinated by the contents of the abdominal cavity laid bare, by the musculature of the chest with protective layers peeled back, by shaded arteries in the shoulder stretched like tendrils of a branching tree, by a grinning, noseless side view of a skull.

This is what we are inside, I told myself. This is what resists when we press against our skin. I thought of my relatives who lived alongside me in the white house. Grand Dan's kidneys were safely boxed in behind her apron strings. My unsuspecting parents, Phil and Mr. Holmes, even my sister, Ally, walked around with trickily camouflaged coils of intestine looped behind their abdominal walls. I contemplated the word *splayed*. I believed from my private studies that the frontier between inside and out was narrow indeed, that there was little to keep my own organs tucked neatly inside: liver, pancreas, stomach, spleen. In my opinion, the heart took too much space and crowded the lungs. The windpipe, cut open, resembled a slashed hose. Fat cells, disguised by the name adipose, were shaped like Aunt Fred's diamond ring, the one she took off when she washed and rinsed the plates in the enamel dishpan.

On the pages of *Gray's*, exposed tendons of the face and throat were ghoulish. The upturned chin and bared muscles of the head were frightening enough to make me think of Miss Grinfeld, who refused to die and mercilessly taught eight grades for decades in our one-room school, with no inclination to retire or to be replaced by a younger, kinder version of herself. She had taught our mother and our aunt, and she lay in wait for Ally and me as we marched into her classroom on the first day of school, September 1932. Ally was in third year because she had already attended school in town, but I was in first. Having discovered Grandfather's anatomy book, I at once transferred my memory-image of the ghoulish throat to the profile of my teacher.

Grand Dan approved of my obsession with anatomy and although she no longer practised midwifery, she might have hoped that I would someday involve myself in the care of the human body as she and my grandfather had done. She was fond of saying, "Be not ignorant of any thing in matters great or small," a theme often heard while Ally and I were growing up. Even so, there were matters great and small that were not discussed. About the matter of sex, the adults around us were vague or silent. Mr. Holmes avoided all reference to the topic and, perhaps because of him, our mother followed suit. I learned more from Grandfather's medical texts than I ever did from my parents.

Diagrams of the reproductive organs were vivid and graphic on the pages of *Gray's* and I had a desire to discuss their perplexing detail with someone. Ovaries, uterus, a frightening-looking vagina, testes, prostate, penis. Because these were called "the organs of generation," I believed, for a time, that only one generation in each family was endowed. I finally asked Grand Dan about this one morning while she was wrapping her legs, and she sat back in her chair with an expression I hadn't seen before. It was an unexpected and momentary glimpse inside her, which I caught before it disappeared again. Her voice was softer than usual when she replied.

"Georgie," she said, "women are made one way and men another, but their parts are meant to be complementary." This confused me, but I kept quiet while I thought of body parts paying compliments to one another. "As it happens," she went on, "men and women come in different shapes and sizes. And when God designed the human body, he ensured that our women's parts were different from men's."

I liked the word *design*, which was enough to satisfy me. I also liked knowing that I was included in "our women's parts." But Grand Dan had taken the question so seriously, I was put off and didn't ask for more.

I went back to *Gray's*, slowly progressing from diagrams to labels, sounding out names of body parts like a mantra, trying to figure things out. I was not exactly certain what the organs of generation did but I knew instinctively that I'd be better off keeping further questions to myself.

My favourite of all the diagrams was the upright skeleton itself. All bone and no flesh, missing part of its head, this erect *Homo sapiens* was ready to rattle its bones and strut out the side of the page. I named him Hubley, having decided it was a he. "Structure determines function, Hubley," I said. "Be mindful of how you behave."

Between September and June, *behave* was something we were forced to do by the ever-looming Miss Grinfeld, who kept strict order in our country school. She was responsible for instruction in every subject because she was the only teacher—all eight grades being captive in one room. We listened to one another's recitations. Younger children read blackboard work written for older children. It was easy to skip grades just by paying attention. Still, Miss Grinfeld managed to celebrate learning. She had ways of persuading us to memorize grammar, spelling and math. She used song, rhythm and a wooden pointer banging against the floorboards to "make the learning stick." She was a purveyor of words and never once did she stab her own foot.

"One and one are two," we chanted as we stood beside our desks. "Two and two are four." Our voices rose robotically, righteously. "Eight and eight are sixteen. Sixteen and sixteen are thirty-two."

She taught the names of the Great Lakes by having us repeat: "Every Man Has Socks On—Erie, Michigan, Huron, Superior, Ontario." She reasoned that there was one *s* in desert because we'd want to cross a desert only once, but a double *s* in dessert because we would want two portions of dessert. She loved the way the English language glued itself together from many eras, many tongues. She spoke with reverence when she discussed prepositions. She wrote them on the blackboard and had us sing them alphabetically, in verses, to the tune of "The Farmer in the Dell." One more song to belt out, though we had to twist our tongues around the rhythm.

About above across after
Against along among
Around as at before behind
Below beside besides

Between beyond but
By down dur—ing
Except for, from in into
Like near—next of off

On onto out over past round
Than through throughout till
To toward under unlike
Until unto up upon with
And without

The last line was anticlimactic but, in a perverse way, we waited, shouting out the two words like grand punctuation marks we'd that moment discovered in the farmer's dell. I didn't know what a dell was, and had to look it up in Grandfather's dictionary at home, but that did not affect the learning of the song.

Memory has not failed me.

My ribs are stiff, but I don't think they're broken. If they were, surely it would be difficult to breathe. My bottom feels the way it felt in winter when I was a child, when Grand Dan and our mother sat Ally and me on a frozen quarter of beef purchased from Mott. The weight of our bodies was supposed to steady the beef while they sawed off steaks with the cross-cut saw. Not wanting to wait until Mr. Holmes returned from the store in town—they knew they were capable of doing anything he could—the two women dragged the side of beef from the summer kitchen, which was used for cold storage from December to March. They laid it on newspapers on the table, covered it with sheets of waxed brown paper, and spread an old coat overtop. While they sawed, Ally and I bounced up and down, on and off the carcass, and yelled, "Are you finished yet? Will you hurry up? Our bums are freezing!"

Which is the way I feel at this moment. Bum is numb and I need to shift position.

Sitting on a frozen side of beef provided one good reason for Ally to hate winter, but even before that she dreamed of living in a warmer climate. Perhaps it was something she had read, or something she'd heard at school. She was convinced that "south" would be an improvement over Ontario winters. "We could move south, Georgie," she said, as we climbed down off the carcass. "The whole family. We could start by renting a villa and work our way up. Do odd jobs. Anything. We could pool our money and buy a place."

"Then what?"

"We'll rent rooms at one end of the villa and live at the other end. Everyone will have something to do. That's how it works in life—haven't you figured it out? Every person in life gets a function. Mother will keep the books because she's used to stretching the money. Mr. Holmes can look after security and shout away intruders. He can also barricade the villa against storms. Grand Dan will cook. If it's too hot to light the stove, we'll buy her a hot plate. And she can deliver any babies that come along. Our four cousins can join us if they want to. They'll be in charge of maintenance. Uncle Fred will inspect their work—and hold their heads under the pump if they don't do a good job." We laughed uproariously. "And he can tell ghost stories after dark.

"Aunt Fred will wash dishes, and sing country-and-western to entertain us. She can also start a fight when we get bored. You can be peacemaker. And set the table," she added, as if the additional assignment of practical work would convince me. "You can also tend any bones that get broken. Put on splints. Grand Dan can wrap them with her cottons."

"What will *you* do?" I was surprised that she had everyone's functions figured out.

"I'll lie in the sun and get warm. I'll read aloud to everyone—and be in charge of good cheer. I'll draw, and maybe sell my art." She looked away. Despite her dislike of winter, Ally had a drawer filled with pencil-crayoned drawings of snow: our stone fence, its outline buried but distinct beneath waves of white; the tilting shed with white drifts sliding into its angle of leaning; the swollen surface of the creek with a spring skin of ice.

"Every household needs a lady," our mother piped up. She was on her knees in front of the coal stove, shaking down the ashes before the steaks were cooked. She stood, and hung the shaker on its hook.

Ally was not deterred. She laid her plans, adding, deleting, adjusting. But I was in no hurry to go anywhere. Nor was anyone else. And no one was more shocked than I when, sixty years later, my beloved sister and her husband, Wade Trick, packed their bags and moved south to Florida.

Scapula

TWELVE

Whoever is in charge of this rescue, please hurry up! I'm not an eighth of the way to the car, which is what I'm aiming for. Car as refuge. Car as haven. Car has a horn. Horn could save my life.

Courage, Georgie. Don't be morbid. It's only a matter of time.

I'm losing track. I'm old and stiff. An old stiff. Come on, bones, don't let me down!

It wasn't so long ago that I read about a woman who lived alone in the country and fell backwards into her own garbage barrel and couldn't get out. Her head and arms stuck out, her feet stuck out, but the rest of her was tucked down inside. She was rescued after several days—alive. The humiliation must have been unthinkable.

There should be something I can remember about survival, something from books. We had a pamphlet on survival in our home for a long time—it belonged to Harry. I leafed through it after he died, and packed it off to a book sale. *Cover the head and neck*, that's all I remember, probably because the words were in bold print. Cover with what? Surely the advice was meant for someone stuck in a snowbank in winter.

Grand Dan said one day when we were sitting in her kitchen—it was a Saturday in the fall and Aunt and Uncle Fred were visiting—"When I'm finished with life, take me out to the back forty and shoot me." Which made the adults laugh, while Ally and I and our four cousins looked on and wondered. Grand Dan wasn't exactly stern, but she didn't laugh that often. When she did, the laugh came out quietly, as if it had been locked inside the soft part of her chin.

That was the day I learned to tie my shoelaces. To everyone's shame but my own, I had resisted learning. Grand Dan sat me on a kitchen chair outside the back door and told me I was to stay there. My cousins ran off to play in Mott's field without me. My fingers fumbled, my thumbs got in the way. Grand Dan demonstrated twice and said, "You may get off that chair, Miss, when you can make a bow that won't come undone. You're a big girl now, and you have to learn and that's all there is to it."

I struggled; I fought off tears of frustration. Ally came outside and sat on the step nearby, for support. The screen door opened and out came Uncle Fred, carrying another kitchen chair. He had huge ears but he laughed about them and told us that *Herr Gott* had provided him with big ears so that he could hear the voices of his four sons, no matter how far they wandered. *Gott* was our uncle's name for God, and he pronounced it like a truncated version of *goat*. He added the *Herr*, he said, because it attracted God's attention.

Uncle Fred pretended not to be able to tell Ally and me apart, and maybe he really couldn't. When he called out "Girl," we both looked up. Maybe, being the father of four sons, he liked to say the word *girl*. It didn't matter, because Ally and I forgave him the denial of our individuality. He did not, after all, hold *our* heads under the pump. And we loved his stories.

After he'd set his chair beside mine, he put a cigarette between his lips and struck a match against the chair-bottom, whipping the flame out from under his seat. A breeze puffed out the flame. He lit another and that, too, went out. Each blown match increased his craving, but he finally gave up.

"Do you see that, Girl? *Herr Gott* is sending me a message," he said, and pointed to the sky. "He knows that I'm trying to give up smoking." He tucked the unlit cigarette behind one big ear. "Keep tying your bow while I talk," he said. "I'm going to tell you a story."

I propped my feet on the rung of the chair, I swung them back and forth, I leaned forward over my shoe and tied a bow, first try.

I've never forgotten the pleasure, the sense of triumph. I did not shout, or run to the house to show Grand Dan, or get up off the chair, which I was now permitted to leave. Instead, I tucked my feet under me and waited.

Uncle Fred grinned. "Aha! You see, Girl, you could do it all along." He looked at Ally and me as if we were conspirators, and began.

"When I was eight years old, not much older than you are now, I travelled on foot with my father to a town on the banks of the Salzach—a crisp, cold river in the old country. So beautiful, you could not imagine." He swept his hands through the air, to show the beauty in his mind's eye. "Salt was shipped down the river before the railway was built. My mother gave me bread and cheese and sausage—*Wurst*—to carry for our lunch. When we reached the town, it was night and rain was falling, and my father found a room at an inn. The place was gloomy, but there was one room left, a corner room, upstairs.

"The bed was narrow, but we both fit in and pulled an eiderdown—a feather blanket—over us. I was tired, and fell asleep at once. My father told me later that he was still awake when he heard a loud thump behind the bed. The thump woke me, and my father whispered, 'Stay quiet. Listen.' So we lay on our backs under the eiderdown and the noise started again, one big thump and then another. There was nothing behind us, no window, no shutter, no place for anyone to hide. My father got up to look under the bed but it was built on a platform of solid wood and there was no space beneath. He got back into bed and we pulled the cover up to our ears and tried to go back to sleep. This was impossible because, right away, the foot of the bed started to move. The whole bed frame began to shake—so violently, I thought we would come flying out and land on the floor. My father said, 'Don't move, don't do anything. We'll see if it stops.' After a few minutes it did stop, but then we heard a bang and the bed began to shake again. Not only that, but I felt a hand pushing on my shoulder. I was frightened, certain that somebody must be standing beside the bed. But there was no one. My father must have been frightened too, because he said we should leave the bed and sleep on the floor. If a spirit wanted the bed, we shouldn't argue. He spread our coats on the floor beside the door in case we had to leave quickly, and lifted the blanket off the bed so we would be covered. We lay on the floor the rest of the night and after that, we were able to sleep.

"In the morning, we were cramped and stiff. We went downstairs for breakfast and my father told the innkeeper—a big man with a big belly—what happened. The man frowned and said there were sometimes ghosts in that corner room. They were from a long time ago, two men who had once fought over the bed. One man was killed and the other died soon after, but they were still fighting. They didn't like anyone else to sleep in the bed. They hadn't been around for a couple of years, the innkeeper said, and he wasn't happy about their return. We never went back to that place, and I was glad to leave the ghosts behind. But I tell you, Girl, while I was lying there, the b'Jeezus they did scare out of me."

Uncle Fred's laugh came out in a big splurt. "Don't worry," he said, "there's no ghost here. If a ghost dared to come to this house, your Grand Dan would knock its block off."

Grand Dan came outside at that moment to check the progress of my bow. She must have heard the end of the story, because she said, "I don't want you scaring these girls, Fred." But it was too late. For a long time, fearing that an ancestral spirit might scare the b'Jeezus out of us, Ally and I refused to go upstairs alone after dark, especially on nights when the adults were sitting around the radio downstairs, listening to the eerie sounds of the creaking door on *Inner Sanctum.*

I hear a scratching from a tangle of bushes. My right shoulder is a board of knot; I dare not think about how mangled it must be. I'm so rattled, I can't think what the shoulder bone is called. But I know other bones—I once knew them all. Shoulder girdle: left clavicle, right clavicle. Humerus.

Did you read the survival pamphlet, Harry?

I'll be a no-show at the airport and Air Canada will give my seat to a standby. Case will be at the theatre and suspect nothing. I insisted on driving myself so that no one would have to go to the city to pick me up on my return. Is this my punishment for being independent?

I'll have to send an apology to Lilibet. I'll be thought rude.

My mind is moving in circles. Mistress of sequential disarray, that's what Harry called me.

Ally and I marched in circles when we were children, around and around the rug in the parlour, singing as we marched.

Onward Christian soldiers
Marching as to war
With the Cross of Jesus
Going on before

If only I could rise now, and stomp up the side of the ravine.

Singing makes me tired. My voice is hoarse. I can hardly speak, let alone shout the words. Scream. I scream, you scream, we all scream for ice cream.

Is Lilibet serving ice cream for dessert?

Grand Dan did not scream when she drove the blade of the axe into her tibia. The women who came before me have set a high standard.

Think, Georgie, think of your plight.

My plight. The only plan I have is a vague plan to pull, push, drag myself. If I could inch up the slope on my back, well and good. But I'm at the bottom; I'd use every bit of energy I have.

I'd die along the way.

Still, I've moved again—not much, granted. But even this small bit has given me a new perspective. The tree above me has had its day, but I see that one side hasn't parted with its bark. It's patterned in whorls like a painting by Emily Carr— all dusky browns and ashen greys, but never bland. I went to a Carr exhibit once, with Ally, before she moved south. We drove to the city and stood in the main room of the gallery, surrounded by fir trees and totems and heaven and light, and pressed our shoulders together and were silent.

And now, I grit my teeth, bear the pain. My head has agreeably parted from the thin ridge of rock. But my leg feels as if it is swelling. I might never walk again. I'll be nothing but a burden.

Keep moving. Reach out as far as you can. Explore with your good hand.

The oak. A tree I know, which makes me quietly weep. Harry and I admired it during our walks, an old friend. We gathered acorns in the fall and told each other it was the oldest tree in the ravine. Its scaly bark breathes; I can set my palm against it. "Builder oak, sole king of forest all."

Memory is holding. Miss Grinfeld would be proud. But Miss Grinfeld has been dead for years, and she and Harry never met. He only heard my stories.

I'm close to the main path. I must be, if this is the same oak. Which might be considered a miracle. Especially if someone decides to descend. Even though it's only April and early for spring hikes.

Small or large, a miracle is what I need.

MIRACLE WOMAN STAYS ALIVE, RESCUED FROM SPINNEY'S RAVINE.

I don't think a rescue is going to happen.

A rescue will happen. You can be sure of it.

I've peed my pants. What will I say to my rescuers?

Don't dwell on it.

Herr Gott, do you mind sending someone down the path to find me?

Please.
I forgot to say please.
I won't ask for anything more.
If I sound like a beat-up songstress, I'm sorry.

THIRTEEN

I've been in and out of sleep; a rustling in the bushes gave me hope. I thought someone was coming down the path but it's a chipmunk scurrying past, headed in the direction I would like to go. It comes to a quick halt and stills. Its tail curves up and back and then straightens like a tiny bone. Why does its stillness look so meaningful, so intent? And now it darts into the underbrush, gone. I should have grabbed that erect little tail, hung on for dear life, let it drag me up the path to safety.

I'm losing my mind.

I was dreaming about my mother. She was sitting in her walker at the Haven, watching the doorway, waiting for me to come to collect her for a trip. Then, we were in the front seat of the car and I had my arms around her as we sailed over the cliff.

Phil did not exactly like the Haven when she first moved there, but she made it clear that she wasn't moving in with me. "I have no intention of being a burden," she said. "Anyway, you'll soon be joining me." I was dismissed. And she did raise a valid question about my own future.

It was the ad "Independent Living" that convinced her to choose the place. I saw that she'd had the plan in her head for months, possibly years. It was raining the morning she phoned, and I held the receiver while I stared out the window at cardinals swooping back and forth from feeder to ravine. I missed Harry and was feeling, yes, sorry for myself.

"I'm moving to that flat-roofed seniors' residence on the other side of town," she said. "The one they call the Haven. A woman just phoned to say that someone died in the night. I was next on the waiting list and had to give an answer, so I said yes. I'll have my own space, a two-room suite. I've been given three weeks to sort out my affairs and I'm going to need you to sell the house."

I'd been given my orders. Ally had moved away, and I was the one available. Phil expected me to do the work, conveniently forgetting my own age. When you have a centenarian mother, concessions will be made. I did not know that she had applied to the Haven or how long she'd been on the waiting list, but she'd always been secretive and I didn't pry. I organized the move of furniture and the listing of the house. She had a chauffeur—me. She had someone to order around—also me. I managed to sell the house the same day the ad went in the paper.

After that, it took Phil two and a half weeks to shed belongings our Danforth ancestors had accumulated over a century and a half. Except for the first six or seven years after her marriage to Mr. Holmes, she had lived in the same house the better part of a hundred years. And she was letting go. It had become too much for her, though she wouldn't admit this. She had to turn her back, in order to move on.

At the time the house was sold, it had already been absorbed by the town and was surrounded by rowhouses that had sprung up on the site of our old field—the one Grand Dan sold, strip by strip, to Mott, when we needed the money. I was saddened to see the past dismantled, but I knew I could not move back. To Phil's credit, she lasted in the house long after everyone else died or moved away. Not that she was alone; the house remained at the centre of the community that sprang up around it. The main road and our own short lane were paved. The only barrier that kept her neighbours at bay was the low stone wall built by our ancestors who had bent to pick stones, one at a time, and thrown them onto a stoneboat as it sailed across the field behind a team of horses.

There was a lightness to Phil, a new-found energy and purpose while she packed. She labelled her belongings: papers, documents, things she wanted to keep—oak table, dresser, bed, two chairs, cabinet, lamp. She emptied closets and drawers and told Case and Rice and me to take what we wanted. Ally wasn't around to help herself, so I set aside Grand Dan's silver, which she had asked for.

After that, Phil began to set out what she called "bric-a-brac"—unmatched dishes, ornaments, linens, pots and pans—a few at a time on the uneven surface of the old stone wall. At four in the afternoon she laid out a teapot with two cups and saucers. By six they had disappeared. She lined up a coffee urn with matching mugs at bedtime, and those were gone by morning. She played cat and mouse with her neighbours and parted with objects she'd owned for a century. She refused calls from dealers. The neighbours gathered water carafes, pressed-glass toothpick holders, fruit nappies, costume jewellery, side tables, porcelain trivets, turkey platters, brass fixtures, a coal scuttle and a collection of small glass hats. Case kept some of the smaller furniture for her theatre. She and I had already removed the books. The medical texts that had belonged to my grandfather, including *Gray's Anatomy*, came to me.

But all the while, I had the worrying feeling that Phil was preparing her exit. Not of her house, but of her life. The morning I drove her to the Haven she began to have second thoughts, and so did I. She looked smaller than usual as she pushed her walker through the entrance. The first person we laid eyes on was an elderly woman who was asleep in a wheelchair near reception. Her mouth was open; her chin rested limply on her chest. A drawsheet was fastened beneath her armpits and tied at the back of the chair to keep her upright.

Phil drew back. "The wheelbarrow cometh," she muttered, looking to her future. Her voice betrayed a quiver of fear as she glanced around. "Everyone here looks ancient."

I put my hand on her shoulder and felt the curve of her back, the prominent hump. I wondered if I should sit her down on her walker and push her right back out to the car. "Are you sure you want to do this?"

"Of course I'm not," she said. "Wait till you're ninety-nine and see how you feel."

The moment for escape had passed; the receptionist came forward to greet us.

I went back to visit every day for the first three weeks. Until Phil met her gentleman friend, Tall Ronnie, she nearly wore me out.

"They serve skim milk in the dining room," she said at the end of the first day. "That's what Mott fed to his pigs. I'm not drinking any skim milk. And the nurses shout at us as if we're deaf. They spend their time with bed patients and rarely check the rest of us who live in the suites. We could die of inattention and no one would ever know."

"I check," I told her. "I check every day."

But I was thinking, what if, someday, Case has to start checking on me? What if she forgets? What if she never checks?

If only she would check now, phone the hotel, see if I've arrived in London. Which I might never see.

Don't allow bad thoughts, Georgie. Maybe she's phoned already.

She won't phone. I told her not to. I don't report to Case.

Never mind that. Think of how long you've been here. Someone might have raised the alarm.

Maybe I've been here only a few seconds. Maybe I'm in one of those time warps I've read about and never understood.

Then pay attention.

FOURTEEN

My chin and one eyelid receive a cool breeze. I hope the temperature doesn't drop, though there are worse ways to die than rotting in a ravine. Think of Isadora Duncan, strangling on her own scarf. Think of the scarf caught in a rear wheel of an open car, whipping her out and tightening around her neck until she had no more air.

Not a pleasant thought, Georgie.

It's difficult not to think unpleasant thoughts. Think of Tolstoy, breathing his last bit of air in a station master's shack beside the railway tracks. He ran away from his wife, gave away his possessions—but only after living his life as a wealthy man. He must have listened to the resolute chug of engines as he lay dying. Did he think of Karenina? His last words were said to be, "It's all so simple." Something like that. At least he finished *War and Peace*.

The library in town couldn't keep me supplied with books. I read novels, history, philosophy, attempts at proofs for the existence of God. How easily I remember those younger years, but with no age attached. It's strange how I don't think of myself as old, even staring at my face in the mirror.

I volunteered as a shelver for years, so that I could be first in line for the new books. That meant finding books for Case, too, when she was a child. "Bring me lots, Momma," she said. She directed, even then. Once she knew how to read, she went through as many books as I.

But what was it that Tolstoy understood? What was so simple? Did he know something the rest of us don't? He slept with serf women, had an illegitimate child—maybe more than one. An unacknowledged son had to drive him around in a carriage on his estate. How fair was that? Tolstoy ran away when he was older than I am, in his eighties. He must have been ready to die. Maybe he'd had it—with his wife and his life.

Well I'm not ready to die, not yet, nosirree. I'll be around as long as my bones hold me up.

Why, then, do I feel as if everything is out of control? If I take my last breath in this ravine, I hope Case won't choose one of those ready-made verses supplied by the *Wilna Creek Times*—footprints in the sand, soughing breezes, that sort of thing. She has imagination, she can create something original; she works in the theatre, after all. Her own theatre. The first and only live theatre in Wilna Creek. She bought the old Belle movie house, got rid of the pigeons, tore out the insides and rebuilt. That was before Harry died. Oh, she's efficient, our Case. But does she ever pause to look around? I don't ask. She's too busy getting things done. Still, she has a vision; the theatre is hers, every board and nail.

Harry and I went to the opening. People came from all over the County, and every ticket was sold. Case had us sit third row centre, best seats in the house, she said. Next to me, on my right,

a man whipped out a tape measure from his pocket and measured the distance from his kneecap to the seat-back in the row
ahead. He had high, bony knees and I thought *patella, patella.*
He looked at me as if to challenge, but I refused comment. He
was a stranger, from away. I did not tell him it was our daughter's
big night, that Harry and I were the parents of the new owner
of the Belle. I did not say aloud, as I might have, that bringing a
tape measure to a theatre was a picky thing to do.

The play Case had chosen was *Waiting for Godot,* a play I
still haven't read. A pair of tramps sat on a chair under a tree
most of the evening and scarcely moved. I wondered about
her choice for the opening, but the actors did make me laugh.
Those two, Gogo and Didi, whatever their names were, waited
and waited and then a new day started and nothing had happened since the night before and they'd gone nowhere. When
it was over, I had a strange feeling of understanding and not
understanding. The self-appointed theatre critic wrote a grand
review in the paper the next day.

But while I was watching, my mind drifted, and I thought
about how my Case and Lilibet's Charles had come so far and
had adult lives of their own. Born the same year, their lives as
complex as any. I thought, well, Case has studied and tried different things and had one partner and that didn't work, and
she left him, and then she met Rice whom she loves, and now
she owns her own theatre and here we are at the opening. And
Charles had a marriage that didn't work and he has a new partner too. A new-old partner. And I thought, *Well, Lilibet, maybe
everything really does come out in the wash.*

Sometimes I find myself thinking about child-Case right
along with adult-Case, and I wonder if Lilibet does the same
when she thinks of her four. Here we are, all these years

later, standing back and watching our grown children have their lives—through ordinary times, through heartbreak and anguish. But even after horrible events—Diana's death was one of them—we are sometimes blessed with a moment of unexpected joy. We learn to grasp, to hold tightly to these moments for the short time they exist.

Seeing Case at the grand opening of her theatre was one of those moments. Her smile could not be erased. Her black hair shone. And after the clapping had ceased and everyone had taken their bows, she had the spotlight come up on Harry and me in the audience, and asked us to stand while she thanked us for our support. When everyone filed out, including the patella man, Harry and I sat back down in our seats, and held hands, and were quiet.

I don't for a minute believe that Case understands the way I see her present against her past. I once tried to explain, but maybe I didn't explain very well. For me, it's impossible to think of one without the other. Child. Adult. Adult-child, a contradiction in terms. But Case moves too quickly to get into discussions of this nature. She solves problems, chooses plays, directs. She doesn't want to humour a mother who can look inside her past—the last thing that interests her right now. But it will, it will. For now, she is part of the theatre. I love the language she uses; I love the way she takes for granted the sense of belonging in her own arts world. It's a little family unto itself.

Maybe she'll choose haunting flute music to drift over my coffin. Or a stirring elegy. Or jazz with a beat trickily played. Like Django, who plunks and vibrates "I'll Never Smile Again" with his scarred and charred fingers until you think one elongated note will break your heart. Except that it doesn't. At the end, you feel mellow and uplifted. Or after hearing him strum "New York City," you want to stop what you're doing and run all the way to New York as fast as you can, on the tips of your toes.

Case and Rice are childless. When they first met, perhaps they made a decision to stay that way. It wasn't discussed with me, but it's a decision I silently mourned. Maybe they mourned, too. There are things Case doesn't share with me, nor I with her. It's understood that there will be no one to follow. She will impart what she knows through her theatre, her art.

She told me one night that she had fallen in love with Rice's mind. I love him too, but that's because he loves my daughter, and because of his music. Case finds ways of putting him and his jazz guitar on stage, or has him play for receptions, or during intermission between acts. He's easygoing, does his own gigs around the County, especially during summer and fall.

It was Rice who told me about Lully—another awful death—though I should stop contemplating death while lying on my back beside a half-dead tree. Lully was a composer in the French court of Louis the something, hundreds of years ago. He used a sharp-ended wooden pointer to conduct and banged it in rhythm against the floorboards. But he became excited and struck his own toe, and ended up dying of gangrene. Lully could have been saved, Rice said, but he was obstinate, he refused to have his toe amputated. Rice sipped his tea. We were in my kitchen, talking about death the way people do. Rice calmly raised and lowered his fist as if he were banging Lully's stick and conducting Lully's musicians. It made me think of my old teacher, Miss Grinfeld, banging her wooden pointer, but I didn't interrupt. They'd heard my Grinfeld stories—or Case had—countless times. And Miss Grinfeld had never hit her own foot or contemplated gangrene.

Rice told me about Webern that night, too. Webern stepped outside onto an Austrian balcony to smoke a cigar in the dark and was shot three times by an American soldier. I thought of Uncle Fred, from Austria; I thought of my father, who died the same year as Webern, 1945, before Case and Rice were born. But the composer's was a quick death, a sudden one, and my father's was not.

If only I could laugh. Stop thinking about death. Keep my thoughts from multiplying. I can't seem to hold back this endless supply. Thinking of Diana's crash didn't help.

I want to drag myself again, but I'll be in danger if I move. Somehow, I know this. Disequilibrium. I felt it when I suffered from vertigo for an entire week last summer. On the third day, Case drove up the hill to see me, her take-charge self exasperated at my self-diagnosis. I was sure the cause was an inner-ear infection, but she disagreed. "Come on, Mother," she said. "I'm taking you to the doctor—and please don't argue." She drove me to my doctor's office and, when we arrived, I crawled on my hands and knees from the reception desk all the way down the hall to the examining room. Case looked away; she hadn't anticipated this. "If you can't walk, crawl," I told her. "If you can't crawl, slide on your bum."

The doctor said I had an inner-ear disturbance caused by a virus; there was nothing to do but wait it out. Case drove me home again and I had the grace not to say I told you so. She helped me into the house and said, "Please, please, do what the doctor told you."

The next day, I stood in the shower and tried to shampoo my hair. I'd been told not to shower because of the danger of falling. I tipped my head back to rinse, and my arms flailed out to save me. I shouted into the air and went down as if I'd been thrown. I stayed on the wet tiles until I was rinsed, crawled out on my hands and knees, yanked at a towel and dried myself while I was still down. I stayed there another half hour, and did not tell Case about the fall. When I stood, I wrapped a towel around my hair and turned my turbaned self to the mirror. I grabbed the edge of the sink, only to see that my shoulders had humped when I wasn't looking.

Like Phil's shoulders.

Can these belong to me? I asked.

My thighs were already bruised, and looked like hams.

Can this body be mine? This face? My expression was Phil's in an earlier decade. And yet, I felt thirty-five inside, maybe forty. I could not see the face of someone in her eighth decade.

Maybe Case will start looking like me someday. Maybe we all turn into our mothers if we live long enough.

I'm trying to be positive. Think of native women, pioneer women who slept out in the open, close to where I'm lying now. In cold and sleet, with or without shelter. Bitten by insects, frightened of howling wolves.

But they didn't have broken bones.

They might have. You don't know that.

The shoulder. Scapula! What a splendid boost is memory.

During all the years I studied the makeup of the human skeleton, I told myself that if Grandfather Danforth had returned from the war, he'd have been pleased to know that his youngest granddaughter had memorized the bones. That she missed his presence and would have loved him fiercely, if only he'd been around to meet her. She might even have learned to be a doctor, like himself.

But he did not come home. And because my father, Mr. Holmes, died after I finished high school, at a time when the dry goods store was floundering, there was no extra money and no possibility of attending university to study anything.

And now, scapula is the last bone I can dredge up.

Backbone

FIFTEEN

My life unknits as I lie here. How many days? How many nights? My stories are my mother's stories, my grandmother's, my daughter's. I did not plan any of them; they became what they became; they are what they are. I look to my left and see the last thin bit of light wobbling through the branches of a high white pine. The tip of the tree is so remote from where I lie, it might belong to a parallel realm, one in which I play no part whatever.

I am not used to perpetually staring up. The side of the ravine is more layered than I imagined it to be. Dusk has sharpened its outlines. Each heavy rock fits the ones above, beside and below, as if laid by the hands of a stonemason.

I see now that I might die of thirst, not of clots or broken bones. My tongue could split in two. The way it has swelled inside my mouth, it might halt the flow of air. I must think of other things if I'm to survive, if I'm to see Case and Rice again. But I have to get water. I've sucked the buttons. What more can I do but lie here like a useless person—the most humbling part of all.

I hear a noise. It makes my ears perk, my heart jump. Rabbit? Raccoon? I'm not fond of things that crawl; they have their place and I have mine. I don't bother them unless they enter my house and, then, I sweep them out.

Still, the noise might have been human. *Hope leapt; hope plunged to the slough of despond.*

Memory spills its lines. The night refuses to be silent. I have to tighten my sweater, gather my coat. If the moon would show itself, I'd feel less alone. How this old root that keeps me company must have groaned when, having once been decently buried and alive, it was pried unwillingly up through earth.

Slowly, silently, now the moon
Walks the night in her silver shoon

I doubt that Monsieur de la Mare ever spent a spring night in Canada on the ground, nowhere to look except at sky. I needn't mention thirst and broken bones. It's terrifying to think that I might die from the cold. Thank heavens for this unusual weather. It was almost balmy when I left for the airport. But cold from the ground seeps into my legs, my bottom, my back. Still, it could be worse.

There. I've looked on the bright side.

I would like to see the moon. Cold company, but company nonetheless.

There was something in the poem about silver paws. Or silver claws. I didn't understand the word *shoon* when I memorized the lines for class. I was puzzled, embarrassed to ask, afraid to be humiliated. Was it sheen, shoe, a pair of shoes? Miss Grinfeld assigned the poem to the fifth grade every year, but most of us had already learned it after hearing the older students' recitations four years before, and three years, and two and one.

Our father liked the poem and asked me to read it for him one evening. I stood beside his chair and recited without looking at the page. He closed his right eye, his left eye hidden by the patch. His brows flattened in the middle and made a single, shadowy line. Mr. Holmes liked tranquility at home, probably because he was not a natural socializer and was forced to greet the public at the store all day. It did not help that when he smiled, his chin tightened in a way that made his smile look like a grimace.

In the evenings, he asked Ally and me about our homework and sometimes demanded to see our scribblers, requiring proof that we were learning. He peered over our shoulders, but never parted with a word of praise. Ally and I did what we could to please him, but he was distant, he withheld. After her homework was finished, Ally turned to her drawings. Across the kitchen table, her hand furiously pencilled and shaded. Mr. Holmes looked at the drawings, picked them up one by one and laid them down. He nodded, but did not speak. I was certain a smile would break out. I tried to will him to smile, for Ally's sake. But he didn't. Later, Ally declared that she didn't care whether he praised her art or not. If he wasn't interested, she wouldn't invite him south when she left our bitter winters behind. She still hated the cold, but neither of us could have predicted then that she would spend half a century plotting her escape.

"We'll find someone else to do security," she said, trying to pretend that I was included in the planning. "Uncle Fred can take that on as an extra duty, and do inspections, too."

I knew that the two of us would have given an entire villa for a word of praise from our father. But praise was not forthcoming and we were learning to pull away from that yearning part of ourselves.

South was no more than a word at that time; it did not have a place name attached. But within a few years we were referring to Ally's villa as "Boca." During several recesses, she had stayed inside to examine the school atlas. She chose Florida, that long lever of land that dipped into the ocean like a notched handle that could be tightly grasped in order to tilt the entire continent on its Alaskan nose. She ran her finger down the Atlantic edge and chose Boca Raton, near the bottom. When Miss Grinfeld had us fill in blank maps of North America, Ally covered the Atlantic Ocean and the Gulf with seagull-wing waves to show water on either side of the long handle she had chosen for her villa.

By then, we were no longer calling her drawings "art." These had become her "work." Decades after our father died, long after she really did move to Florida, Ally told me on the phone one night that she was certain Mr. Holmes had been emotionally dyslexic when we were children. "We just didn't know how to describe it at the time, Georgie," she said.

I wasn't entirely convinced about emotional dyslexia, but I did know that our father had spread gloom throughout the house when he was in it. And now, all these years later, I have only a feeling of sadness, a feeling that something was wasted, something that might have been.

At night, our father shouted in his sleep, and in every room he could be heard. "Keep away from the ribbons! Bolt the door! Get away from the till!" On and on it went. Someone was after him. Someone was robbing the store. When his shouts woke us, we rolled onto our backs and stared at the ceiling. Sometimes we whispered to each other, wondering if the night train had passed through town and out the other side, heading towards us. There was no clock in our room, but if the shouting occurred close to midnight, we would soon know the exact time. At three minutes past twelve, the long thin wail of the whistle drew close. The sound widened the air through which it tunnelled, sailed across Mott's darkened field and into our room. It provided comfort from the blackness of night, relief from the tirade coming from the next room. It gave us permission to go back to sleep. I pulled the covers over my head.

During the day, as if to counteract the spreading gloom of Mr. Holmes, Phil was cheerful around Ally and me. But we sensed the necessity for split allegiances. There was a clear dividing line between Mother and Father that Ally and I did not cross. "Why did they marry?" we asked each other. "How did they meet?" But we had no answers and were afraid to ask. There was already enough to worry about without adding to existing problems.

Phil did not make a fuss about the night shouting except to say, one Sunday morning at breakfast, that she was glad our father didn't sleepwalk, too. Mr. Holmes flatly denied talking or shouting in his sleep. Grand Dan remained neutral.

The noise again. A rabbit would be easy prey down here. I know there are foxes; Harry and I once saw an undulating brush slip into tall grass and disappear in the dusk. We also came across the bones of a snowshoe hare. And there are grouse, wild turkey; they won't hurt. Bears don't come this close to the edge of town. Thankfully for me, there are no wolves any more—not in this ravine.

One day in early spring, Ally and I found a dead kitten beside the banks of the swollen creek that ran along the edge of Mott's property. The temperature had dropped dramatically the previous night, and the day was one of dry, blue cold. We held our breath, took tentative steps on the surface crust of snow. It was a heady feeling and I recall the satisfaction of knowing that my boots would not punch through. We both saw the kitten at the same moment and leaped down the bank towards it. We could tell it had been in water because of its clumped and frozen fur, and we told each other that someone had tried to drown it and had tossed it in the water farther up the creek. It had managed to drag itself out and up the bank but despite the effort, or because of it, the sad creature did not survive. It died with one eye open. "Like Lazarus," we said, as we carried it home between our mittens and dug through a layer of snow in an attempt to give it a burial. Lazarus had risen from the dead and maybe the kitten would, too. We used a pick from the shed, but the pick sprang off the frozen earth and made our arms shudder as we took turns digging. We buried the kitten more on top of the ground than below, and packed tight snow around its corpse.

Ally complained while she swung the pick, her scarf ends swaying. "I'm getting out of here," she said. "I hate winter and I'm moving south, to warmer climes." I knew the word *climes* had come from Miss Grinfeld. She was the only person who would use such a word in ordinary speech, and I admired Ally for making it her own. Later that week, I watched across the table as Ally made a drawing of the dead kitten, half in and half out of the creek, its open eye unseeing. The unbroken snow upon which we'd walked had a lustrous, rippled sheen, as if providing a background of glory to the site of the cat's demise.

The following Sunday, Ally and I read to each other in the kitchen. We were required to read aloud from the Bible every Sunday afternoon for twenty minutes—Grand Dan's rule—and we took turns handing it back and forth, doing our best to search out interesting passages, loving the sound of biblical language.

Thinking of the kitten's shallow grave, I read, "They found no more of her than the skull, and feet, and the palms of her hands." I quickly altered *hands* to *paws*.

When it suited our purpose, we made certain we were overheard. Another Sunday, while trying to convince our parents that we needed new shoes for school, Ally read in a loud voice, "How beautiful are thy feet with shoes, O prince's daughter." But there were no new shoes. Not during the years of the Depression.

When it was my turn to read, I thought of Sog, a chubby boy in Ally's grade who'd earned his nickname by bringing soggy tomato sandwiches to school for lunch. Even the paper bag that held them had wet patches. At recess, Sog told Ally he loved her, and on the following Sunday I read, cryptically, "At her feet he bowed, he fell, he lay down." We laughed as if we were possessed. Neither of us was interested in love. Not then.

"Lazarus did stinketh," Ally read aloud.

We marvelled, not only at the miracle, but at the word *stinketh*, which we incorporated into our private lexicon. When we carried garbage out to the refuse pit at the back of the property, Ally held her nose and shouted, "This is disgusting! The whole place doth stinketh!" When a squirrel got into the root cellar and died, we were told to carry its rotting body outside on a shovel. "Truly," we complained, "this bringeth no amusement."

At night we lay on our backs in our double bed and invented sentences for thither and nay and doeth and smite and belongeth. "Shew us the door," we mock-read one Sunday. "We wisheth to play, and desireth fresh air."

A firm response came from the next room. "It behooveth thee to read until thy time is up. Then shall thee be shewn the door."

But Lazarus did stinketh—or so the Bible said.

What did Lazarus learn the second time around? That's what I wanted to know.

Grand Dan's Bible readings were from Ecclesiastes, which she freely quoted and which I learned, by listening. "You're the one with the memory," she told me, as I followed her around and recited: "To every thing there is a season, and a time to every purpose under the heaven."

Ally and I read other books besides the Bible, any books we could find. I was making slow progress through Grandfather's fifteen volumes of Dickens, my favourite being *Great Expectations*. Another of my favourites was *The Princess Elizabeth Gift Book*, which Ally—not I—had received for her birthday from Aunt and Uncle Fred. I resented this because I was the one who'd been born the same day as the Princess of York. But no one else recognized the slight. A book was to be shared no matter whose it was. This book came into the house not long before the abdication, after which Lilibet found herself in direct line for the throne.

Every adult we knew had something to say about the abdication of King Edward VIII, one of the great-grandsons of Queen Victoria. *It was a tragedy. It was treason. It was an honourable act because he had the backbone to stand up and claim his lady love. He didn't want to be King anyway. He didn't have it in him.*

The town, busy preparing for Christmas, was quick to pledge allegiance to His Majesty, George VI, the new king. "We shall rally round and give him our support," the mayor declared.

In our one-room school, Miss Grinfeld stood at the front of the classroom beneath a sagging bell of green crêpe paper, which the tallest of the grade eight boys had strung from the ceiling the week before. She bowed her head and wept. At recess, I heard her mutter, "Oh Eddie, Oh Eddie." She had had a glimpse of him when he was still the Prince of Wales, during his two-month tour across Canada after the First Great War. In January, when we were back at school again after Christmas holidays, she read the "Message of Abdication" aloud, in its entirety, and wept again.

The women of the town were bereft. They came into the store and spread even the tiniest bit of news, which our father sometimes brought home. The customers had believed in the Prince. They'd loved him. But he had chosen Mrs. Simpson of Baltimore with her cool, cameo profile. He sailed from Portsmouth on board a destroyer and left the mother country behind. He landed at Boulogne and entrained for Vienna and went on to the castle of Baron de Rothschild in Austria. Later, after Mrs. Simpson's divorce, they married. But she was no princess, said the women of the town. She wore a long narrow dress with a plain skirt, and a hat with no veil that could be seen. She was so thin, she resembled a rib that had been straightened at both ends.

Ally and I had never heard such a fuss. But long before the Prince made his public declaration, I was enamoured of *The Princess Elizabeth Gift Book*, with its plethora of princesses. The illustrations were of girls entirely unlike Ally and me, and this might have been the attraction. They wore cream-coloured dresses with flowing skirts, their laps strewn with pink roses. There were drawings of bears and dolls and giant puddings. Both Ally and I read and reread the stories and poems, and silently studied the illustrations. Each time Ally closed the book, she returned to her drawings of snow. When I closed the book, I felt as if I had travelled to other lands.

Come and change, come and change
Into anything you will

I recited the lines when we were outside. I loved make-believe, to a point, until it interfered with my practical side. Genes which I believe Case has inherited. Ally told me, long after we'd grown up, that she still experiences a physical sensation when she thinks about our days reading the *Gift Book*, a deep sense of dreaminess and longing.

SIXTEEN

I've slept again. I dreamed of Lazarus, of water dripping from a tap. Has an hour passed? A minute? My body is tightening, shrinking from the cold. Clouds lie on their backs like sullen bears. How do they stay aloft? Grand Dan sat in her chair on Sundays with her Bible on her lap and read, "He that observeth the wind shall not sow, and he that regardeth the clouds shall not reap."

But what is this? Tears?

Rain on my face. Soft, and oh how welcome. A gift from the sky. It must not be wasted, not a drop. I've tried not to allow myself to dwell on thirst but now I can admit how little hope I've had, how parched I've been. Hold out my good palm, suck my fingers, scrabble for a dry, downed leaf, a blade of last year's grass, suck the edge of my sweater. A crazy woman I am. When I grope and scrape with my hand, bits of shale loosen around me like handfuls of pennies. But my fingers are wet, my sleeve holds moisture. And I am thankful.

Little drops of water, little grains of sand.

How things fly into my muddled brain. I'd heard this recited by Grand Dan at home, and one morning at school I tried to convince Miss Grinfeld that the line was a sentence. She was teaching nouns, banging her pointer and chanting "Person Place or Thing!" and making the class repeat after her, "Person Place or Thing!" She did this for three consecutive days, telling us that the chant would never leave our heads. For the rest of our lives, we would always be able to identify a noun.

But *my* words, she argued, after asking me to construct a sentence, did not make a sentence at all. My words had no predicate. She stood over my desk.

I resisted. Nothing she said could persuade me to understand the meaning of the word *predicate*. She gave up and turned to the other students. I looked at her back and silently rolled off my tongue, *Little drops of water, little grains of sand*. I loved the sound, loved the line. Sadly, it did not have a predicate and therefore was not a sentence. I did not like Miss Grinfeld that day. I gave up the soothing sound and went home after school and opened *Gray's Anatomy* and stared at the ghoulish throat that resembled my teacher.

Miss Grinfeld had every country child in her grip for eight years. She filled us with warnings about stepping on rusty nails and the threat of lockjaw. I lived through a mercifully brief period of being terrified that my jaw would clamp shut through no fault of my own and that no one would be able to pry it open, not even to give me water. She did spot checks of our health habits, made us confess what we had eaten for breakfast and admit whether or not we'd brushed our teeth before we walked to school. While we were eating lunch at our desks, she wandered between rows and peered into lunch buckets and honey pails into which were tucked roast-beef-and-radish sandwiches, or scrambled eggs on four slices of bread. In late spring, when we ran out of jam at home, Ally and I watched in dismay on the days Grand Dan prepared our lunches. We exchanged glances that meant "Sugar-sandwich day" and looked on glumly while she dampened her homemade bread with milk and sprinkled brown sugar between the slices. By the time lunch hour came around, the sugar had dried, and it scattered in every direction as we lifted our sandwiches to our mouths. Miss Grinfeld walked past, her chin defining a circle that followed the pattern of brown dots. It was humiliation of the worst sort; our dresses were speckled from neck to waist. We never spoke of this to Grand Dan.

During health class, I did not let on to Miss Grinfeld that our mother could faint at will, because I was certain she would call this a family peculiarity, like being born with lumpy cheeks. Our teacher sat erect in her straight-backed chair and described generations of chinless families, implying some sort of bad behaviour. She told us not to let our bottom jaw hang open because doing this made a person look stunned, as if gorilla laughter would spew forth. We were quick to pull up our chins in class, but when we were out of earshot in the schoolyard we drooped our jaws and forced chortles from our throats.

Every spring, Miss Grinfeld stood behind her desk and declared that this was the day the bees began to swarm. She taught us to be suspicious of adults who cooled their tea in their saucer before drinking—something Uncle Fred did every time he visited, though I did not betray him. I also said nothing about him wearing a freshly pressed shirt to bed every night, one that he had to iron himself.

Before we arrived at school each winter morning, Miss Grinfeld had already placed a cod liver oil capsule in the pencil groove beside the hole in our desk that held the inkwell. We were required to swallow the fishy-tasting capsule before the day began, and she stood in front of the big boys and made them open their mouths in case they'd stored it in their cheeks to spit out when her back was turned.

In our last year, before she sent us off to the town high school in Wilna Creek, she insisted that during the month of May we memorize an entire Shakespearean play, even though this was not on the senior curriculum. She alternated year by year between *Julius Caesar* and *Macbeth*. In my final year, it was *Macbeth*'s turn, even though I had learned *Julius Caesar* by paying attention to the seniors' recitations the year before. In fact, for one month of the school year, every child in our one-room school could recite at least some roles, line for line. That we often did not know what we were learning was of no consequence. The truth is, most of us loved the sound of the parts we memorized and, for a few short weeks, these were shouted out in the schoolyard at recess.

But *Little drops of water, little grains of sand* did not have a predicate and was not eligible to be a sentence.

Part of me is dry; the branches link to protect. I'm familiar now with their pattern, a soft and purposeful webbing. That small bit of water has revived my spirits. Even so, my tongue is stuck to itself, my gums and lips cracking. I'll raise my sleeve again and suck its dampness. I must collect more drops. The sweater will absorb more if I pull back the coat. But I don't want to freeze. The temperature could fall and I might not be rescued before nightfall. My face is in the open, but I still have a way to go.

I hear a car on the road above and realize I've been listening to the sound of tires on wet pavement. Fellow humans, so close, what comfort. Maybe it's Pete from the cul-de-sac at the end of our street, or maybe Pete's wife. Pete walks in the ravine, but it's still early, only April. I have no way of attracting attention. I'm out of sight. Invisible. Too far down. The flesh will fall from my bones and I'll become a female version of Hubley the skeleton. I'll be here all summer and fall. Snow will cover me, and Ally will draw a long bony digit pointing through a crust of white. No, she won't. Because I'll be out of here by then.

Cover your head and neck.

If only I had a blanket to pull over my head. I've nothing to cover myself with. It's the cold that needles away at my flesh, a slow, steady stitch. I'm lying out in the rain. I don't deserve this. And I'm crying, a wasted effort, I know.

Where's your backbone? You've sucked your bit of water. Keep your mind alert. Follow a thread. Move your body again.

If I could listen to music, I'd feel better. When Django played, he was always hurrying. Plinky-fast, a reassuring beat. He played at out-of-control speed, as if his music accompanied not body, but spirit. It was as if he knew he had to move quickly if he was to squeeze in everything there was to do.

Never mind Django. Drink. Take in every drop you find.

WISHBONE

SEVENTEEN

I'm seizing, involuntarily. I have to clench and unclench my fingers, painful or not. I have fought off arthritis for years, even though I'm frequently reminded that muscles and bones have tricks of their own. After Harry died, while I listened to jazz in the evenings, I pulled at my fingers, opened and closed my fists, tried to keep my hands from tightening.

Metacarpus. Carpus. Pisiform—in the wrist—named for its likeness to a pea. When I found this in *Gray's* and showed it to Ally, the name made her blurt with laughter. We weren't allowed to say pisiform in the house; it was deemed to be an indecent bone. That's the kind of family we had. Our bones supported us, but some were not to be mentioned.

Until my car dropped off a cliff, my bones gave me wondrous support. Like the rubber jar rings that held up the brown-ribbed stockings we wore to school. Did we really wear those around our thighs? It's hard to believe. It's a wonder our legs weren't gangrenous by the time we were ten. Phil and Grand Dan pulled at the flat red rings, softening them up until they could be stretched into garters. Ally and I rolled them over our feet and worked them up our legs, and walked around all day with lumpy circles beneath our skirts. Did we have toothpick legs?

Because of falling sales during the Depression, Phil had begun to work at the store in town, three days a week, alongside Mr. Holmes. She was worried about the long hours he was putting in and did her best to absorb some of the workload. She darted around the store, moving quickly between counters stacked with neat bolts of cloth. She had always liked to sew and, when business was slow, she slipped easily into the duties of filling order sheets for flannels and unbleached cottons, drapery material, millinery felt, mourning veils, hat wire and trimming. Mr. Holmes sold sundries, too: ribbons and threads, needles and pins, hooks and eyes, buttons and cotton tape measures. After Phil began to help out at the store, she ordered garter elastic and that put an end to rubber jar rings around our thighs.

Phil was enjoying her days in town, and occasionally stopped in at bazaars or rummage sales when she took a break from the store. One day she brought home a slightly tattered book called *Queen of Home*. For a time this rested on the lower shelf of the oak table in the parlour, the one that held the glass-leafed tree. Tree on top, book on the bottom. Grand Dan laughed when she saw the wine-coloured cover with gold embossing—she had known the book in her youth. It had been published in the 1880s, which Ally and I believed to be the dark ages. We had no idea what was still to come in our own century.

The book was intended for women who reigned over their households, and I suppose that described the combination of Grand Dan and Phil in one house. I came home from school one day to find thick curtains hung across every open doorway. Phil had read a chapter that said all doorways leading to a hall should be curtained with double velour. Velour had not sold well at the store, so she'd tucked bolts of it into the car and brought it home and hemmed it and hung it up. Grand Dan agreed to the change because she did not want icy drafts in winter causing us to become ill with "the shivering fits." She kept her own supply of turpentine and goose grease in the pantry for those occasions.

Ally and I were required to do more housework now that Phil worked at the store, and this meant that we had to stay inside to learn to appreciate the power of elbow grease. As seriously as Grand Dan doled out the chores, we made light of them. When we dusted, we sang. If we were told to wax and polish floors, we wrapped thick rags around our slippers and shuffled across hardwood, bumping hips every time we made a pass around the room, batting at the velour that blocked the doorways.

At night in our bedroom, Ally sometimes read aloud from *Queen of Home*, which was about the proper way for a young couple to set up house. She had not yet assigned the housework duties for the villa in Boca, and we were determined that neither of us would be stuck with a mop and bucket in hand.

I knew some of the dialogue by heart: "*I hate housekeeping, answers the young wife.*"

Ally piped up: "*Pardon me, please, but if this be the case, you have no right to marry at all.*"

This made us laugh out loud, even though we were beginning to think that perhaps we did want the right to "marry at all." Not then, but someday.

Grand Dan did not help out at the store, but she kept up the garden in the yard. When we came home after school in late spring and early summer, she was often outside, planting or watering or tending to the wagon-wheel garden that encircled her rose bushes. In no time at all she had us both weeding, one of our after-school chores. The garden was important to all of us. We were living through the Depression; there were few extras on the table, despite our parents doing everything possible to keep the store running and money coming in.

Ally and I tried our own hand at being providers, the summer after our mother began to work in town. In early June, unexpected company dropped in late one Sunday afternoon and had to be invited for supper. There was no extra vegetable to serve with the meat and potatoes that we always had. Butterbeans weren't ready; lettuce had not come up. From the kitchen window, I watched Grand Dan go outside and kneel between rows, where she began to tug up her tiny baby carrots. While she was destroying her own garden, I thought of her reciting: "A time to plant, and a time to pluck that which is planted." I was certain I had seen her wipe her eyes. A half-hour later, when the carrots were served—small and stubby as knuckle joints—I refused to eat a single one.

Because of seeing Grand Dan weep, I devised a plan later in the summer and persuaded Ally to join me. Peas were grown on the farm past Mott's and, at harvest time, the wagons had to travel the main dirt road to get to the canning factory. We stood in the veranda until we saw a team of horses approach, the wagon behind stacked with peas as high as a load of hay. We ran out to the road and waved up to the driver and a second man who sat on the wagon seat beside him. A hot dry wind was blowing, and there was a good deal of noise from the rattle of the wheels. We began to chase the wagon, and ran alongside, ducking down, grabbing at vines, dropping them as we ran. We were hot from running, and laughing from the sheer craziness of stealing. The men could see us perfectly well, and one of them craned his head back and shouted down at us from the wagon, but we couldn't hear because of the noise. Ally was doubled over. I looked at her hands full of pea vines, her wrists drooping, and I thought of the wrist bone in *Gray's* that was likened to a pea and I shouted "Pisiform!" and Ally understood and shouted back.

"Pisiform!" we yelled at the top of our lungs. "Pisiform! Pisiform!"

We hollered into the hot wind and aimed our indecent bone at the wagon, and the men looked back and smiled and waved. We stopped running and laughed and laughed and tried to catch our breath and retraced our steps along the road to pick up the vines we'd dropped. Each of us had a huge armload and we carried the tangled mess around to the back of the shed, where we separated pods and chucked peas into a bucket, eating while we worked. We were not prepared for Grand Dan's reaction when we carried the peas triumphantly to the house. "They fall off the wagon anyway—sometimes," we said, in our own defence. "And the men didn't mind— they just laughed at us." We did not mention hurling our indecent bone.

But that was not good enough. Our punishment was to sit outside on the stoop and read the Ten Commandments aloud. Even so, the five of us dined that night on every stolen pea. And good-for-nothings that we were, in the bottom of the serving bowl, we left an extravagant puddle of melted butter.

EIGHTEEN

Yes, we stole those peas. I would steal water now if it were reachable. I own a kitchen sink, a tap, a shower, a tub, a garden hose hooked up in the backyard. And what do I have to show for myself? Cracked lips and damp clothes. Store-bought clothes that are thick enough, but my veins and my bones are chilled through and through.

The clothes Ally and I wore were homemade, though we longed for store-bought. Phil and Grand Dan were creative about piecing together leftover bolt-ends from the store, plaids and solid colours, odds and ends of velvet with wool, rickrack trim on cottons. Even so, I have a distinct memory of being held together precariously. During high school years, a cache of safety pins was kept on the kitchen windowsill so that Ally and I could solve last-minute problems of missing buttons and sagging hems on the way out the door. Later, during the war years, when we had no nylon stockings, we drew pencilled lines down the backs of our bare legs, practising on each other. We were beginning to be on the lookout for love.

We swapped jewellery, exchanged blouses and sweaters, added and removed collars and belts, painted our toenails and left a half-moon. Despite being younger, I was two inches taller than Ally, which meant that she could not wear my skirts. At thirteen, I was five-seven and growing, and acutely aware of the fact that I had inherited Grand Dan's genes for long bones—she was five-ten, long and spindly. I opened *Gray's* to recheck the femur, which stretched the length of a page, top to bottom, and resembled a club that could be swung through air. When I did stop growing, I was a half-inch shorter than Grand Dan. I was comfortable with my height because of Grand Dan's example, but felt unusually tall when someone short stood beside me. Whenever this happened, I inched off sideways, like a crab. I did the same at the community dances, held at the church hall.

I'd been attending the dances from the time I was six years old, when we first moved to the country. The hall was adjacent to the Anglican church, and children attended along with everyone else. At the first sound of the fiddle, a man whom you wouldn't expect to have a hope of staying in step would put a hand to his partner's waist and, with a straight-armed push, steer her around the room as if she had no more substance than a Bernhardt scarf. That was how light you felt, if you were the woman. If you were on the sidelines, what you saw was a roomful of men, faces earnest and intent, going about the business of pushing their women around the floor as if they were featherweights. You'd think foot patterns had been laid over the wooden floor, because everyone danced exactly the same way: seventy-year-olds, high school students, children, young couples, widows, widowers. After the start of the war, we knew that soldiers and sailors and their girls in the towns and cities were learning the new dances. But country dances stayed the same and that is a fact. Every person in the County knew the two-step, knew how to square dance and how to face off for a Virginia reel. Even our father danced—in the years before he became ill—and that was something, Phil's short body being pushed around by the unsmiling Conrad Holmes, easily spotted on the dance floor because of his black patch, and rumoured to be a German spy because of his first name, even though the *Conrad* part did not start with a *K*.

The only person who did not dance was Grand Dan, although she attended and sat on a hard-backed chair at the side of the church hall. "There's a time to dance, and a time to mourn," she told me, with a nod that meant she was quoting from the Bible. Publicly, she neither danced nor mourned. It was simply understood that no man dared to stand before her and proffer his arm. Grand Dan's legs had been bandaged since she'd received the War Office telegram—from the First War, not the Second—and her feet no longer danced.

She loved music, however, and listened to dance music on our big radio. We all did, especially on Saturday nights when we sat in the parlour listening to Guy Lombardo and his band, broadcast from the Roosevelt Hotel, hundreds of miles away in New York. Ally and I sprawled on the rug; Father stretched out on the sofa; Grand Dan and Phil sat in armchairs. No one said much, but there was foot tapping and occasional shoulder swaying. We glanced up at one another every now and then. Most of the time our eyes were focused on some vague spot on the rug. When I think back to this—could it have been a single moment?—I think of peace, even happiness. The picture stills; it is complete. This was the family I'd been graced with. This was where I belonged.

James Cagney, too, danced during the war years. He danced up the walls at both ends of the stage in *Yankee Doodle Dandy*. When the movie came out in the early forties, I saw it twice, at the Belle—the same theatre Case now owns. I was with Ally the first time. The second time, I returned alone for a matinee, just for the pleasure of sitting by myself. I wanted the moment before the velvet curtains split at centre stage; I wanted the pause before the lights went down. I wanted to watch the talented Mr. Cagney dance across the stage. No one thought of him as a dancer, but I did then and I still do now. So much energy in one small body. Such an unlikely looking man for being so light on his feet. I didn't care so much about the *Yankee Doodle* story or what happened next, though the story was good enough. Even the sounds of the knitters behind me, their needles clacketing in the dark as they knitted socks for the boys overseas, could not ruin my enjoyment. I was there to see Cagney dance.

Lives had been changing since the beginning of the war, and changing quickly, everywhere we looked. Older girls Ally and I had known from school were leaving for the city to take up factory jobs, and were allowed to wear trousers to work. Older boys were enlisting. This included Wade Trick, whom Ally swore she was going to marry at the end of the war. She had known him since high school, and he'd been one of the first to sign up. After he left for overseas, he wrote to Ally every week, and told her he was learning a trade in the army. He would soon be a qualified electrician and said that when he got home it would be easy to find a job. She immediately wrote back and assigned him electrical duties in Boca, putting him in charge of dealing with power outages after hurricanes. She still had not assigned the housework duties, but she wasn't worried. She said she'd find someone eventually.

Wash floor after dark
Bring sorrow to your heart

Who said that?

Grand Dan. I heard her voice just now. Uncle Fred believed in spirits, and so can I.

Grand Dan truly might have believed that everything turns to sorrow. She had lost her husband to one war and then watched Phil—and all of us—lose Mr. Holmes at the end of the next. The women were queens reigning over the household, but men headed the family; there was no disputing that. Many people believed that households headed by women were not meant to last.

The store did not recover from the Depression and business did not improve after the war began. Because of his age and his blind eye, Mr. Holmes had not been able to join up. He was sensitive about his German-sounding name, and took extra measures to proclaim his loyalty to the citizens of Wilna Creek. Not that anyone doubted his patriotism; he frequently donated a portion of the store's meagre earnings to war causes. In the main display window at the front of the store, he went so far as to put up a large government poster that portrayed a huge white elephant. A tiny man and woman at the bottom of the poster peered up at a For Sale sign tacked to the elephant's side. The elephant had a placid but jolly expression on its face and the caption read: IF YOU DON'T NEED IT, DON'T BUY IT. People on the sidewalk frequently stopped to look up at the elephant, and from inside the store I saw them nod their heads as they moved on and did not stop to shop.

To display such advice was not sound business practice, and I overheard Grand Dan say to our mother one morning, "He's shot himself in the foot, Philomena. The man has shot himself in the foot."

Grand Dan telephoned Mott and asked him to drive her to town. She walked along the sidewalk to my father's store, stood for a meaningful five minutes outside the window, and stared in around the edge of the giant elephant, to prove her point. She did not enter the store, but neither did Mr. Holmes remove the poster. Citizens of Canada had been urged to be mindful of extravagance, to buy bonds, to save waste paper, not to gossip, to still our tongues. Mr. Holmes wanted to prove that he was as loyal as the men who marched up the street in uniform with bands playing behind them.

He brought home printed instructions to save waste bones, because bones could be made into glue for aircraft. To please him, we promptly began to drop chicken bones and ribs and thighs into a pail with a lid. The pail had to be kept outside the door because of the stench, and animals came round at night. Phil fainted one day when the lid was left off. Despite my ana-tomical interest, we stopped saving bones because we had been given no advice about where to send them once we'd amassed a collection. Ally and I buried them at the edge of the refuse pit, and shouted as we dug, "Pit and all do stinketh!"

One afternoon, while our parents were at the store, Aunt and Uncle Fred arrived unexpectedly. They planned to stay overnight and had left the boys at home, with the eldest in charge. When Uncle Fred came into the house, he produced a bottle of dark rum, which he called "Nelson's Blood," from his Gladstone bag.

"Come here, Girl," he said. "And bring some glasses to the table." Ally and I brought glasses, but every one of them was chipped. He picked one up, ran his finger around the rim and set it down. He picked up another and did the same.

"Well, that's it," he said. "We're going shopping. Get in the car, Girl."

Ally and I both climbed in, happy to have a drive to town. He took us to the grocery store, where he walked up and down the pickle aisle and put eight jars of mustard into the cart. Each jar was shaped like a drinking glass; each was decorated with diamonds, hearts, spades and clubs, and had thin red and black lines painted around the rims. Uncle Fred paid for the mustard, drove us home and asked for a mixing bowl. He pried off the lids, emptied the eight jars of mustard into the bowl, took the glasses to the sink, rinsed them out and shelved all but one in the kitchen cupboard. "There," he said, pleased with his own ingenuity. "Now you have a set of glasses and a full bowl of mustard, too." He poured himself a drink, had a minor fight with Aunt Fred about the mustard jars—"Why didn't you just go out and buy a set of glasses!"—and waited for my father to come home from work.

When Mr. Holmes arrived, he sat at the kitchen table with Uncle Fred and drank a glass of Nelson's Blood.

"Here's to the spirits inside us, the ones that warm our bellies," said Uncle Fred, and they clinked mustard glasses. There was an air of precarious jollity in the room.

I believe Father liked the rum, though he sat stiffly, like a soul conflicted. Even so, he seemed to enjoy the story Aunt and Uncle Fred had to tell. On the way to our house, a great fight had taken place on the King's Highway. They knew every pee stop on that highway, between our town and theirs. They knew where the washrooms were clean and where they were filthy, where to find homemade raisin pie and where the spice cake was stale. Uncle Fred swore that the best liver-and-bacon breakfast was served in a service-station diner. Aunt Fred said there wasn't a handle on a toilet she couldn't flush with her shoe.

The fight took place at a pancake house, miles from nowhere. They quarrelled; Aunt Fred shouted, stood up, dumped a bowl of syrup over my uncle's head and walked out. She got into the car and locked the door, but when she started the engine, she remembered that she had left her glasses in the restaurant and couldn't drive without them. Inside, Uncle Fred was wiping syrup off his skull. The waitress brought a damp cloth so he could clean himself up. He left his pancakes, paid for the uneaten meals, scooped up my aunt's abandoned glasses and stomped outside. He circled the car, threatening, until Aunt Fred rolled her window down an inch and then unlocked the doors. At the same moment, she spied a drop of golden syrup that had landed inside one of his huge ears. She hooted with laughter, which made him angry all over again. By the time he was sitting behind the wheel and she had slid over onto the passenger side, the two of them were exhausted. They locked the car and went inside once more, this time to share a pot of tea. They had lost their appetites, and the tea calmed them down. Just as they pulled onto the highway again, the wings of a great blue heron unfolded from the landscape at the side of the road. Uncle Fred was certain that this was a positive sign.

They took turns recounting these things until I asked, "What was the argument about?"

There was silence. Neither could remember. "It must have been something small," Aunt Fred said. She lowered her brows and looked Uncle Fred in the eye, which meant that he wasn't to tell.

"I guess it wasn't important," Uncle Fred said, while we waited for an answer.

But Aunt Fred told me later, out of earshot of my uncle, that she did remember the sensation of risk that had rolled through her like a wave when she held the syrup bowl in her hand and knew what she was about to do. I tried to imagine Phil dumping syrup over the skull of Mr. Holmes, but the image would not be conjured.

After we'd all had our supper, we moved to the parlour so that we could listen to *Boston Blackie*, Uncle Fred's favourite radio program. He refused to miss an episode, whether he was home or a visitor in someone else's house. He and Aunt Fred sat quietly, not a hint of old quarrel in the air.

Before my aunt and uncle left, I overheard my mother telling Aunt Fred how much she enjoyed working at the store.

"I love having a proper job," she said. "Even if I get tired of some of the customers. You wouldn't believe what they find to crab about." Her greying hair was now cropped below her ears. She had bought a pair of glasses and these had small, round lenses that magnified her eyes. She was filled with energy in the evenings, and she had begun to tell stories of her own. Stories about customers who came in and out of the store, what they wanted, what they paid, what they revealed about their lives. Someone's brother, a midget, had grown a foot and a half after he'd had his appendix out. Someone's sister had danced with the Prince of Wales twenty years ago, in Ottawa, and was still talking about it. Not only that, but she had been lucky enough to dance with him twice.

When Ally and I helped out at the store on Saturdays, Phil taught us to cut a straight line through material by keeping our eye on the tip of the scissors. The best way to measure a bolt of cloth was from nose-tip to fingertip, with one arm stretched out horizontally. "It's a yard," she said, as she poked her arm to the side. "A yardstick measure. As long as you don't turn your head." She also began to recount stories of her childhood, when she and Aunt Fred had been children and shared the same room—even the same bed—now shared by Ally and me.

Mr. Holmes, on the other hand, was coming home tired at the end of the day. His fatigue dampened us like a sodden cloak. He made himself difficult to love, but that was one of the facts of our lives together. We knew he loved us, but he was difficult to love back. I wondered why this was so, but there was no one to ask. If we had met our grandparents on the Holmes side, we might have had some insight, but there was no chance of that because they had died so long ago.

I went back to *Gray's* and opened it to see what I could learn about the symptoms I was observing in my father, but I could not match his obvious exhaustion to anatomical description. I tried *Queen of Home*, and turned to the chapter called "The Sick-Room." The nearest advice I could find concerned nervous disorders. Emotions, I read, could wear away the brain. Eight hours at one stretch were sufficient for any man to use his brain. If he exceeded that amount of time he would become nervous and exhausted.

I could not understand why Mr. Holmes was wilfully marching towards disaster. Once home from work, he had supper and then fell asleep, sometimes on the sofa. When this happened, we weren't able to listen to the radio after our homework was done. One evening while he was sleeping in the parlour, he shouted, "Save the buttons! Grab them, quick! Dump them in here!" Ally and I, bent over our scribblers at the kitchen table, looked at each other and shrugged. His face was becoming thin; the patch over his left eye failed to hide dark rings above the bone of his cheek—the malar. I thought of *Gray's* and the yawning hole above the bone, which, on the page, looked big enough to swallow the face of the person to whom it belonged.

I went back to *Queen of Home* and worked up the courage to warn Mr. Holmes, telling him that if he refused to pay attention to the evil effects of the stress of brain work, it would soon be too late. I read out the symptoms as I stood over the sofa: dull eyes, heaviness of head, a stupid feeling after meals. These could lead to insanity and even death. Another evening, I read a different passage, letting him know that if he continued to neglect the warnings of brain exhaustion, he would be considered not only a fool but a criminal. Irritability towards his youngest child became a sudden, new symptom displayed by Mr. Holmes, one not listed in the sick-room chapter. He sat up. His face reddened; his unpatched eye glared. I quickly left the room.

The fatigue of Mr. Holmes, his general state of illness, went on through all the years of the war and became the norm in our home. What I did not know, what none of us knew, was that Mr. Holmes was suffering from chronic liver disease and that he would die in the fall of 1945, only months after the town celebrated peace. Trick had returned safely from the war, one of the first boys to come home. Mr. Holmes was present at Ally and Trick's wedding but he was unsteady on his legs, and his skin and the whites of his eyes had yellowed. He wasn't happy about having to be supported on either side, but he did his best to try to smile at the guests. All of us were pleased that he was not too ill to sit through the ceremony. The night before the wedding, he presided over the family supper table, and a grand feast of roast turkey was served. He carved the plump bird and carefully removed the wishbone, and presented it to Ally, his first-born. She still has it, unsnapped, to this day.

NINETEEN

Rock of ages, cleft for me
Let me hide myself in thee

I sound like the *Titanic*, going down.

It was Mr. Holmes's favourite hymn, and we sang it at his funeral. Five women sat in the front pew: Grand Dan, Phil, Aunt Fred, Ally and I. We wore black dresses, black gloves and black hats with veils. We rose to our feet together and sat down together, and held hands all the length of the pew.

Whenever I recall this day, I always think of the photo of the three queens at the funeral of King George VI. Queen Mary, the Queen Mother and Lilibet were heavily garbed in black, their profiles shadowed by dramatically long veils that flowed over their heads and shoulders. It was apparent that they were grieving but each, by herself, was a vision of strength.

At my father's funeral, the closed coffin was ten feet in front of us, and we stared at it as if fearing that Mr. Holmes would suddenly shout and push back the lid. Our regular minister was ill, and a man who had never met my father was sent from the Anglican church in the next town to conduct the service. He gestured towards the coffin and, in a mournful voice, began to talk about our dearly departed Connie Humes.

Someone must have given him the wrong name. The five of us in the front pew burst out laughing. I kept my head tucked to my chest and told myself we were suffering from brain exhaustion, nervousness, stupidity, grief. We shocked the congregation of mourners—the church was full—and we disgraced ourselves. Uncle Fred, and Ally's new husband, Trick, seated in the pew behind us, could not understand what was going on. We laughed and laughed, and mopped the tears, passing handkerchiefs back and forth, our shoulders shaking and pressed into one another. We were out of control, and hoped that the people behind us would think we were sobbing, even though the minister in front could see perfectly well that we were hysterical. To add to the emotional bedlam, Grand Dan had forgotten her glasses at home and could not see the words of the next hymn—unfamiliar to us and chosen by the new minister. Phil whipped off her own glasses and thrust them at Grand Dan, who tried to hook the wire frames under her veil and over her ears. She looked back at us as if she were going to bleat. We were off again. None of us knew the words, none of us sang. We had been caught out, and we laughed through hard, crying tears.

We sobered on our way back down the aisle and, as we followed the coffin outside, Grand Dan took my arm and walked beside me. We were eye to eye because I had almost finished growing and she had begun to shrink. She muttered in a low voice between her teeth, "There's a time to laugh and a time to weep, Georgie. But sometimes the two get muddled up."

After the graveyard portion of the service and when we had returned to the church hall, Aunt Fred took me aside and told me about the memorial service held for my Grandfather Danforth, before I was born and shortly after the arrival of the axe-bloodied telegram. Aunt Fred was in a remembering mood, having been younger than I when she lost her own father. Because Grandfather was blown up, she said, there had been no body to bury. Even if his bones had been found, they would not have been shipped home from France. It was a funeral without a coffin. The townspeople from Wilna Creek came out to our country church to pay respects. Automobiles, horses and buggies were lined up along the dirt road and side by side in the churchyard. Grand Dan's axed leg was extended straight out in front of her. Every pew was full, and chairs had to be set at the back of the church so that no one would have to stand. Grand Dan sat with her head bowed while she listened to the memories of a lineup of colleagues and patients, and then she laughed with a sudden, short bark. It was as if she were telling them that they knew nothing of the Dr. Matthias Danforth she had loved. She had held him between her thighs; she had run her hand down the muscles of his back; she was the one who made King Edward cake the way he liked it, with walnuts ground into the icing. She knew that he buttered his rolls in the centre and not to the edge, and that he held his knife in his left hand. She was the one with whom he had sat on the veranda in the evenings and shared his concerns about the men and women who climbed up onto his examining table in the Danforth library. She was the one whose skin, under his tracing fingers, had turned to silk. She barked her laugh once more and it was a laugh of pain.

What we were laughing at during the funeral of my father, I now believe, was fear.

TWENTY

We were on our own. Stuck with one another. If we had been largely a household of women before the death of Conrad Holmes, we were now entirely so. We knew this as we bowed heads at the graveside, as we stared down at the coffin in the hole and at one another's feet. Grand Dan's cottons were smoothly wrapped under lisle. The heels of our shoes sank into soft soil. I stood beside Phil and felt her body tremble through her gloved hand. Afraid that she would faint at will, I gripped her arm, but she did not sink to the floor until we were back in the church hall greeting mourners. Most were helping themselves to tea and sandwiches served by the Women's Auxiliary, of which Phil and Grand Dan were members. So natural was Phil's collapse to her knees and then to the floor, I wasn't sure whether she had brought on the faint or if it had been caused by true oxygen deprivation.

Aunt and Uncle Fred stood together in the church hall and did not break into a passionate fight as they usually did when they were in company. Ally and Trick, the newlyweds, held hands. I was pondering my future, which was in a state of confusion. On the way home, Grand Dan sighed as she looked out the window of Uncle Fred's car. "We still have the rest of the hayfield," she said. "That will be our insurance." All of us knew that the store, a business that had been sinking for a decade, would have to be sold. It was also my place of work. Within a few weeks, we came to realize how truly bad business had been. The sale of the store managed only to cover outstanding bills.

Ally went back to her art—she was using charcoal, sometimes watercolours, and still liked to work with pencil crayons. She and Trick had a place in town now, and the first thing I noticed when I visited was a new drawing tacked over yellowed wallpaper in their living room. I recognized our father's store, which, in the drawing, was buried under an avalanche. The roof was covered in white, the entrance hinted at by shadow, the main display window obliterated except for a jagged opening at its centre. Torn, but clearly visible over this central darkness, was the poster of the white elephant, one placid eye staring out.

When Ally came out to the house again for a visit, she and I sat in the room we used to share and talked about our father's death. We began to wonder what his last words had been. We asked Phil, but she became deliberately vague and said she didn't remember. She'd been with him in their bed at the moment of his death, ten past seven in the morning. We found her vagueness surprising, though we didn't press the point. Had he shouted her name? Did he know he was dying? Did he mention us? Ally and I asked each other, but Phil remained silent.

"You'll have to hire a shouter," Ally said to me privately, "or it will be so quiet, no one will get any sleep."

But we did sleep. Gloom had left the house, and the space it once occupied demanded to be filled. The store was up for sale and we prepared for the handover. At home, Phil drew the curtains and darkened the parlour. She walked through rooms slowly, made camomile tea and began to phone old friends, women she had known during her school days and women who had shopped in the store. She accepted condolences and commiserations. And she started, again, to work.

She was already known to be a fine seamstress, and now autos drove out from town and up our short lane. Women in stylish shoes stepped through the back door. They turned slow circles in our kitchen while being measured, and spread patterns over the table, discussing the way they wanted adjustments made. Phil, who now referred to herself as "dressmaker," held a mouthful of pins between her lips while she raised and lowered hems. She stood on a short stool to take tucks under armpits, to let out waists, to adjust bustlines—and she talked about Mr. Holmes.

"He was a wonderful man," she said, through her teeth. She grasped a pin tightly between her fingertips, daring her clients to challenge. "A wonderful man. When he came home in the evenings, he entertained us with stories of the old country. He was learned, too. And brave. He would have fought in the war, except for his eye."

I watched and listened, astonished. Fate had handed Phil the role of widow, and she was going to make the best of it, even if she had to reinvent her life.

The next time I went to town I talked to Ally, who was not unused to inventing roles for her still imaginary villa. "Maybe it takes too much energy to recall darkness and gloom," she said. "Phil probably draws strength from making a new life for herself and consigning Mr. Holmes to a happy memory slot. Like some sort of character in a play."

Indeed, the stories we had once heard from Phil after work each day now became stories Mr. Holmes had supposedly related. The Singer was pulled out farther from the wall. The treadle was pumped over and back, over and back, its regular hum becoming the new noise in the house. The needle stabbed and stuttered through yards of cloth fed into it. Phil cast off her mourning clothes and rewrote her history. She had a long life left to live.

TWENTY-ONE

I've read that our bodies shift forty times a night when we sleep. What happens if we can't move our limbs? Does the blood congeal? I have to resort to kicking the air with my good leg, punching with my good arm. One leg, one arm, one side scrabbling. I've invented the beetle kick. But I'm losing strength. I've been lying here forever, I feel sure of it.

Django was born outside, not in a ravine but in a Belgian field. Rice told me how wonderful music began to come out of him at an early age. When I listen to his strumming, I feel as if he's about to run all the way up a fret and out the other side of my mind. An amazing spirit. But did he also die in a field? I think not. He died on his way home from a railway station in France. That was the year Lilibet was crowned in *her* country, 1953. How earnest she was at the Coronation. More than a hundred of us crowded into the Town Hall auditorium to watch the ceremony on two of the town TVs, set up on the edge of the stage. My Case and Lilibet's Charles were almost five years old.

Yes, railways do play their part in history. Tolstoy dying in a station master's shack; my grandfather, who left on a troop train and never came back. Aunt Fred, who, the Thanksgiving after she was widowed, packed a suitcase full of dark meat from the twenty-two-pound turkey she had just roasted and travelled a hundred and sixty miles by train to bring it to my mother. Aunt Fred ate only white, Phil only dark, and not a scrap of either was going to be wasted. And there was Uncle Fred, who did his own ironing and wore a pressed white shirt to bed every night in case he was called out when a train jumped track, or in the expectation of a passenger and freight train colliding head on and bursting into flames. Uncle Fred, Inspector, was always ready. Aunt Fred refused to iron his shirts—and who could blame her?—when he was only going to wear them to bed.

There was also the Royal Train in 1939—Uncle Fred called it the "pool train"—when Lilibet's dad, King George VI, and her mum, the Queen, crossed Canada and stood on the rear platform in Brockville for one of their scheduled stops. Uncle Fred drove all the way to Wilna Creek to pick us up, and then on to Brockville where he and Aunt Fred, Ally and I stood beside the track—as close as we could get with our uncle's official railroad status—and gazed up at the Royal couple. My four cousins were not present; they preferred to stay home to get into trouble. The Queen wore strands of pearls around her neck, a pearl bracelet, and two puffs of white fur attached like vertical muffs to her sleeves. Uncle Fred cajoled a superintendent into giving up a copy of the train's Royal menu, and Ally and I laughed on our journey home as we read out the choices: *Chow Chow* or *Queen olives, Pressed ox tongue* and *Quince jelly*. But the Royals ate potatoes, too, just as we did. And green peas. They were

allowed pie or pudding or fruit, for dessert. After going over
the menu in every detail, we examined the colour photograph
on its cover, and admired the King and Queen and the two
princesses in their crowns and ermine cloaks, which spilled
down over red, carpeted steps. We settled against the back seat
of Uncle Fred's car, tired and silent, chastened by largesse.

But enough is enough. I haven't lived this long only to rot
on the ground thinking of princesses. If someone doesn't find
me, my skeleton will mould with the oak. Centuries from now,
I'll be a slab of petrified wood.

The cheese in my fridge will be mouldy when I get home.

I might never see the inside of my fridge again.

What will happen to my own fur stole? The mink I haven't
worn for years but never threw away. It was Phil's. She handed
it to me in a brown paper bag, the day she moved into the
Haven. She bought it after Mr. Holmes died, with the wages
she earned from dressmaking. Case has always laughed at the
fur stole. Laughed or shuddered, take your pick. She'll probably throw it into a trunk in the theatre storage room and haul
it out someday for a vintage play.

*Oh stop, Georgie. Keep your spirits up. Someone will be search-
ing. You have only to believe.*

I'm the Mistress of sequential disarray; Harry was right. I
can't keep my thoughts straight for two minutes.

It is deathly silent here, so quiet I hear the flap of a single pair of wings. In summer, Ally and I lay in the field and
watched huge flocks of birds flying swiftly in a single direction.
The birds flattened as one mass and flicked through the air like
cloth, and then, with the same swiftness, veered and disappeared into a slit in the sky we didn't know was there. Where
did they go? A mystery.

If anyone is searching for me now, I'm the mystery. Phil might be seated on her walker wondering why she hasn't heard a word since my arrival in London. I said I wouldn't call until I was back, but she might expect a call anyway.

She'll be waiting for her pigskin gloves.

It has become clear to me that Phil takes her long life for granted, that she plans to outlive everyone, including me. She has already outlived her husband, her sister, her brother-in-law, my husband and her friends. She plans to outlive the other residents at the Haven, whom she collectively calls "the inmates." She has also begun to steal, which, when I was first told, I found hard to believe.

The more I thought about it, the more I realized she'd been moving in that direction for some time. Before she decided to become an inmate herself, she was obsessed with watching crime shows on TV. She kept notes, referred to as "suspicion reports." When she looked out the windows of our old home and saw herself surrounded by newly constructed rowhouses, she began to record any behaviour she deemed suspect. Her reasoning was that she would be a reliable informant if ever called upon to be an expert witness. Because she wrote on yellow sticky notes, these were not lasting testaments. They curled up and were thrown into a kitchen drawer. I leafed through some of them before I advertised and sold the house.

- *Tall young man, black hair, entered corner house. Carried white cloth in two hands.*
- *Woman, royal blue coat (doesn't suit her) canvassed at door. Fraud? Gave no $.*
- *Man in plaid jacket walked centre of road, stopped by stone wall, marched four paces on spot. Lunatic.*

Those are a few I remember.

She steals only on Mondays, sheet-changing day. Six months after she moved in, I was invited by the nurses to attend a staff meeting about her kleptomania. Phil was not present.

"I don't hurt a soul," she said, later—and I suddenly felt weary. I looked at the face of feigned innocence before me and wondered if we'd switched roles and I had become the mother.

"I take things when I'm on my rounds," she went on. "I nip into suites when no one is looking. Sooner or later the nurses find out where I've hidden my cache and it's returned to the owners. No harm done."

"What do you steal?"

"Belts, buttons, combs, a hand mirror—the old-fashioned kind with a bone handle. I stole that from Maudie Hanslow—remember her? She's about ten years younger than I am. She used to come to the store. She tried to tell me I shortchanged her one day, after she bought a tag-end of felt. Well she's an inmate now, and I stole her mirror. Serves her right.

"I also steal chocolate bars—I don't eat them; I just take them. I grab up things that are small enough to stash under my clothes."

She watched my face as she spoke. "It takes energy to steal, you know." She looked at the floor and slumped and then raised her head and added slyly, "You wouldn't believe how boring it gets."

The staff members were not amused. It was reported that Phil had stolen a tin piggy bank from the bazaar table at the front entrance. "The bank," said the charge nurse, "was found on a windowsill in your mother's room. Behind the curtain."

"Why would you steal a piggy bank?" I asked, later. "You have money. Why didn't you just pay for the bank?"

"I did," said Phil. "I dropped a quarter inside and then I stole it."

She was energized by theft.

Oh, Lilibet, did you have responsibilities like these before the Queen Mum died? Were you held accountable? I know you addressed her as Mummy, because I heard you on TV, calling out during a horse race. Did she order you around? At least you were not her chauffeur. There were staff members, weren't there? Stalwart, reliable people to take hold and keep Mummy occupied and well.

I think Phil's friend, Tall Ronnie, aids and abets, Lilibet. I believe he checks to see if the coast is clear. They are a Mutt-and-Jeff pair but I'm glad they found each other. He's almost six feet tall, hunched, while Phil has shrunk to five two bent over her walker. But she can still move quickly. And there's one other thing. Tall Ronnie can't stay in one spot while he's talking. He ends up a foot away from the point at which conversation begins. I have to tell my body to root to the floor when I'm facing him; otherwise, my feet will follow. His head shifts from side to side; he shuffles; he cannot remain still. I finally get relief when he sits, because then his body behaves like that of a normal person.

When Phil first told me about him, she slipped in the information one night just before we hung up the phone. I admit to being surprised, especially as she had never shown an interest in finding another partner.

"Oh, and I have a new gentleman friend," she said. "He's ninety-two and lives across the hall. The only thing I don't like about him is that he cracks his knuckles. This will interest you—I can hear his fingerbones all the way from my room, even when I put a pillow over my head."

She paused as if unsure whether to say more, and then she added, "His name is Tall Ronnie. He offers his arm in the old way. When I go into his room, we shut the door. This drives the other inmates crazy. Maudie Hanslow said, at breakfast, 'I thought we were all past that sort of thing. It's unseemly.'"

I didn't ask.

"Also," said Phil, "Tall Ronnie knows how to make me laugh."

He is as unlike Mr. Holmes as any man can be.

Two

Septum

TWENTY-TWO

I wouldn't be lying here if I'd moved to Boca Raton. Ever since Harry died, Ally and Trick have been trying to persuade me to join them in Florida. But how can I leave Phil? She needs a daughter close by. Even one with broken bones.

If Harry were alive, he would reach out his hand and pull me up.

I could count on Harry. Who wouldn't count on—indeed, who wouldn't want to marry—a man who'd been carried around on an English pillow as a child? Our entire courtship was a celebration, and I could use a few celebrations to think about, right now.

I wore a pale blue suit at my wedding, with a matching pork-pie hat made of felt. How could I have worn a hat shaped like a pork pie? I must have liked it at the time, although I questioned my taste when I saw the wedding photograph, later. I looked foolish; I couldn't think what had come over me when I chose such a thing. Why didn't Ally step in? Or Phil, or Grand Dan? Why didn't Aunt Fred speak her mind?

I'd known Harry a few weeks when he jokingly mentioned the pillow, and my lips shaped the words *satin, tassels, prince.* My head whirled with images of pages in training, curly-haired youths dressed in cream-coloured livery and lined up for the privilege of transporting the young Harry. In my mind's eye, I saw a cherubic boy wearing an oversize turban on his British baby head, a green jewel in the centre of his forehead. He could have walked out of a story in *The Princess Elizabeth Gift Book.*

When Case was in grade one, she asked about our courtship.

"How did you and Daddy meet? How did you know you loved him? How could you tell?"

I wanted to say, "Because of his strength. It filled every room he entered." I wanted to say, "Because of his voice. Such a voice, a voice without shouts. His gentleness. And his shoulder. If you could have seen his sloping, wounded shoulder when he came back from the war." I wanted to say, "Because of the flame that jumped between us."

Instead, I said, "I married him because of the pillow."

"Tell me the pillow story," she said.

Each time I told the story, the details were different. She didn't seem to mind what was fact and what was not. The truth is, I made up almost everything because it was story itself that interested her until, finally, she'd heard every variation I was capable of inventing.

The real story is this. Harry said little about his history until just before we married. He was not a person who talked a great deal, and I believe he was terrified to unearth his own life. But once started, one memory yanked on another until his past spilled out like sheets tied together in an attic and tossed out a window for rescue.

Orphaned in England at the age of three, Harry spent his next four years in an institution on the outskirts of London. At first, his body was weak and undernourished, and he grew slowly. Because he was often sick, the thin, brittle bones in his legs refused to hold his weight—"They were like sticks," he said—and the larger, stronger orphans had to tote him around on a lumpy pillow that had been recruited from a weather-beaten chair in the garden. Harry was a diversion, and the others didn't mind carrying him around.

He settled in as one of the Home Children and was soon able to walk by himself. Four years later, when he was seven, he was sent out to Canada by ship. This was the twenties, not so long after the end of the Great War. In cramped quarters he crossed the Atlantic, travelling with fifty-nine other boys and girls between the ages of three and fifteen. Five adults, their escorts—two women and three men—crossed with them. Each child was given a small trunk and a Bible. When the group disembarked, the children wore name-signs hung around their necks. Some of the children were so young they peed their pants when they were excited. A sailor on the ship showed Harry an open sore on his penis and said it was from "doing it." Harry did not know what "doing it" meant.

The ship docked in Halifax, and from there the children travelled for days by train until they arrived in Toronto. They were met at the station by two women in long skirts, and were led to a house for temporary holding. There was a sign beside the door, but Harry could not read it.

"I never forgot the first meal I had in that house," he told me. "Chicken and potatoes, carrots, thick slabs of bread with lots of butter—I was allowed two helpings—and for dessert, raisin pie." He grinned as if this had been the one truly happy memory of his childhood. He leaned back into the sofa and took a deep breath. "I was safe and my belly was full. But I left three days later and never returned. I wouldn't have known how to find the house or what it was called, even if I had been able to make my way back to Toronto."

Before sailing home to England, one of the men who had accompanied the children on the ship asked Harry if he remembered that he had an older brother and sister. Both children had crossed the ocean several years earlier, preceding Harry to Canada. They'd been sent to the west, and lived on separate farms. For Harry, the story was a fairy tale. He had not seen a brother and sister since he was three and did not believe in their existence.

A farmer had put in a request for a young boy, so Harry was sent on a second train, by himself, to a small station in rural Ontario. He did not know where he was going but when the train made one of its stops, the conductor indicated that he was to get off. Once again, Harry wore his name on a sign around his neck. No one was beside the tracks to greet him when he climbed down. He wanted to get back on the train, but it chugged off, leaving him behind. Eventually, the station master noticed him standing there and gave him a chair to sit on, outside.

"That's when I understood how alone I was," Harry said, his voice becoming softer. "That's when I first thought of myself as an individual. I was seven years old."

I held my body still while he talked, and tried to see the small boy who had never known a time when he had not been surrounded by lineups of other children. He had never been alone, and now he found himself sitting beside a set of iron tracks, with dense and frightening Canadian forest on either side.

"It was the first time I truly thought of myself as *I*," he said. "I looked around and stared into the bush and, so help me, I could not understand why I had no mother. I sat on that chair and cried and cried. I thought my lungs would turn inside out."

The rest was more difficult to hear, but Harry was determined to tell the whole story. Away from Home officials, he was not given a room in the farmhouse, but was made to sleep on a bed of hay in a loft inside a shed. In winter he suffered frostbite, and when he grew out of his shoes, he was not allowed to have another pair. He tied rags around his feet and was given old rubber boots several sizes too large, so that he could work in the barn. He received no pay. He was not permitted to eat at the family table, and was given leftovers after the host family had finished their meal. To make matters worse, the farmer and his wife had a son the same age, and this boy wore proper clothing and was permitted to go to school. Harry was not. He ran away when he was eleven, made his way to the nearest village and was sent back, only to be beaten. He ran away again at twelve and thirteen and fourteen. Finally, no one pursued him and he got away for good. The farmer had had his slave labour for seven years. Harry did not receive a penny for his work.

He followed the railway tracks and walked south for three days, resting and sleeping in fields and barns, drinking out of streams, arriving at a sizable town, which happened to be Wilna Creek, a town he'd never heard of during his seven years of isolation. It had a long main street, a train station and bus depot, a hospital and a number of small businesses. Outside the town were a quarry, several gravel pits and a canning factory. He inquired at the general store and was told that a local farmer named Dixon was looking for help. Harry walked another three miles, this time to the east, and when he turned up at the

Dixon farm he was hired on the spot. He was given room and board and two dollars a week. He was provided with his own room, up over the summer kitchen. He had never lived in such luxury. Not only that, but Mrs. Dixon was a former teacher and after a few weeks she began to teach Harry to read and write. He fell in love with this second foster family and stayed with them for several years, until Mr. Dixon could no longer afford to keep him. Those were Depression years, and there was barely enough to go around. Harry remained in touch with the family, but moved to a room in town and took odd jobs. By 1939, he had earned enough money to buy his first suit. It fitted his lean, muscular body and had a herringbone pattern and cost him twenty-two dollars. Two weeks after the purchase, he joined up. He left the suit with the Dixons when he went to say goodbye, and told them he'd be back. He asked them to look after the suit, because he planned to find a woman to marry when the war was over. That would be me. Neither of us knew the specifics of this; we had not yet met.

When I first laid eyes on Harry Witley, it was 1946. The war was over and he had recently returned from overseas. His ship had been torpedoed off the coast of England and had gone down. He was rescued from the water and picked up by another ship, and the second ship was torpedoed, too. Who, you'd wonder, could have that kind of bad luck? As if that were not enough, a piece of jagged metal had been blasted into his shoulder moments before he found himself in the Atlantic a second time, swallowing salt, shouting for rescue. As proof of the blast, he had an inward-twisting scar, larger than his fist.

He had been treated in hospital in southern England and had recovered enough to work. He answered an ad in the *Wilna Creek Times* for "Young man of character, no experience needed," and was given a job as an apprentice to a Dutch jeweller who had recently moved to Canada and set up shop on Main Street, three doors from the dry goods store my late father had owned. The Dutch jeweller's name was Mr. Ring, which amused people of the town, considering his occupation. He called his shop the Double Ring, after himself and his wife. Mrs. Ring looked after the accounts in a black ledger. She was a plainly dressed woman, but wore earrings that dangled and shone in the light. It was said that all of her jewellery had been designed by her husband.

Mr. Ring's first name was Cornelius. He was a stooped man in his sixties, and highly skilled. He had come to Wilna Creek because a cousin who'd lived in the town since the 1930s had sent a letter to Holland after the war, telling him that the town had a railway, that businesses were opening up, that the place was growing faster than spokes could turn in a wheel.

During the last two years of the war, Mr. Ring had experienced hardship in his country; Harry told me he rarely spoke about this. I found it difficult to imagine the two men, both given to silences, sitting in the shop and having occasional abrupt conversations about the buried past. Mr. Ring was pleased that Harry had been in Canadian uniform, and sometimes told him a little about the Dutch town he had lived in before it had been occupied. He had hidden away a number of diamonds during the war, and it was the sale of these that enabled him to start over. For him, Wilna Creek represented the new world. He and his wife were cautiously hopeful, despite having sorrow in their background. It was rumoured that they had lost someone during the *Hongerwinter*, or maybe to the Resistance. It might have been a daughter or a son; no one knew for sure.

Harry and I met soon after he began to work for Mr. Ring, at a dance in the hall of the same Anglican church I had attended since I was six years old. He and a friend from his boarding house had heard about the Friday night dances and got a lift out from town. He stood before me and asked me to dance. He was slightly taller than I, had a sloping shoulder, and hands with slender fingers. He had a low, husky voice that carried a trace of old England. I took his arm and allowed him to lead me to the dance floor.

Eight days after the dance, on a Saturday evening, Harry walked the two miles from town, knocked on the door, spoke quietly to Grand Dan and Phil, and our courtship began. Months later, after he'd been coming to the house regularly, he showed his scar to Grand Dan and me in the kitchen when Grand Dan asked to see his wound. She was, no doubt, thinking of the blast that had killed her own husband thirty years earlier, and she told Harry about my grandfather's last words and how she had received them. Harry opened his shirt and allowed her to inspect the scar. She looked it over from front and back, and nodded to let him know that he was to rebutton his shirt. She always had a fondness for Harry.

TWENTY-THREE

I must not dwell on Harry's orphan childhood. I felt badly enough when he told me his story, which I thought about for weeks. I mourned the small child who sat on the wooden chair beside the tracks, the abused boy who slept in a shed and suffered frostbite and was not permitted to go to school. I was outraged on his behalf, and despised the adults who had abused him. But those events had happened long before and I had not been a part of them.

Ally was twenty-one at the time of her wedding, and I was the same age when I married Harry. It was 1947, the year after I met him. Lilibet, too, was twenty-one—she and I were married the same year. My wedding was in August, hers in November. We were child brides, all of us. What did we know? What did Phil and Mr. Holmes ever tell Ally and me? What did the Queen Mum and the King impart? I know that on our side of the ocean, we felt a distinct lack of information in the air.

After I married, I thought about this one day when Phil told me a story about one of Grand Dan's deliveries during her time as a midwife. Called to a farmhouse because a baby was on its way, she arrived to find the young woman in the last stage of labour, sitting on the edge of her bed. Convinced that the baby was about to come out of her mouth, she was holding an enamel dishpan under her chin.

Grand Dan removed the dishpan and told the girl to lie down. After the birth, when the cord was cut and the baby cleaned up and rubbed with oil, and after Grand Dan had given the mother a brand new cake of Baby's Own soap, and after she'd burned strips of cloth on top of the wood stove to get rid of the birth odour, she sat on a chair beside the bed and told the young mother what she needed to know.

"She was no more than seventeen," said Phil. "What worried Grand Dan was the girl's confusion about how the baby had been put into her in the first place."

That was the end of the conversation.

The story interested me for a different reason, especially as it had come from Phil. At no time in our lives had anyone thought of imparting what Ally and I needed to know. But there was no point in saying that, not after we were both married. In any case, hadn't Grand Dan discussed with me, once, if vaguely, the matter of complementary parts when I was a child?

When I finished telling Case about Harry and the pillow and our courtship, she looked up and said, "Is that the end of the story, Momma?"

Well, no. I married Harry, after all. In my pale blue suit and my pork-pie hat.

Our father was dead; Ally and Trick were married; I was still living at home with Grand Dan and Phil. A man named Ira had purchased the dry goods store shortly after Mr. Holmes's funeral, and asked me to stay on to do the work Phil had once done—serving customers, ordering fabrics and ribbons, buttons and needles and thread. Every morning, I walked as far as the mailbox, where Mott's son, Junior, who worked at the hardware store, picked me up and drove me to town. I was glad to have a ride in cold weather, and I chipped in fifty cents a week to help with gas. Trick had taken over our father's car, and he drove out to the country on weekends to take Grand Dan and Phil wherever they needed to go.

My employer, Ira, was tall and concave and had a receding mandible. When I first met him, I thought of *Gray's* and Miss Grinfeld, simultaneously. He shaved, but his cheeks were shadowed with bristles. He made me think of consumption, excessive thinness, the crooked letter *C*. When he faced people, he approached and pulled away at the same time. He began his takeover of my father's store by having a huge one-day sale of old stock, and I stood on the sidewalk with Ally and Grand Dan and Phil as we watched bolts of familiar plaids and wools and voile tucked under arms and carted out the door. The former enterprise of Mr. Holmes was, in a single day, transformed.

Before we married, Harry and I had saved enough money to begin paying rent on a small, three-bedroom bungalow in town. We planned to move in when we returned from our honeymoon, and hoped to stay there until we could buy our own house. As it turned out, affording own house took longer than expected; we didn't move up the hill overlooking the ravine until Case had finished high school.

Our wedding took place August 2, 1947, a quiet celebration witnessed by nine people, including the Dixons, the family who'd been keepers of Harry's suit while he'd been in the navy. Harry's legs were wobbly and he complained of being hot in his suit, but we managed to get through the ceremony.

Among other gifts, Phil gave me an electric sewing machine. Ally painted a dazzling picture of the Danforth country house, white surrounded by light. Grand Dan gave us the glass-leafed tree, the "tree of life" that had belonged to my late grandfather. Harry and I had a modest plan to spend a three-day honeymoon in Syracuse, New York, a four-hour bus trip that included the border crossing. Neither of us had been to the United States. I had never stayed overnight in a hotel.

We had hoped to attend the annual New York State Fair, but it had been suspended after the attack on Pearl Harbor and hadn't started up again after the end of the war. Our hotel was close to South Salina and Jefferson, in the theatre and shopping district. I wanted to go to Loew's State Theater, having heard about its elegance, its grand staircase and Tiffany chandelier. We were headed for a big city—over two hundred thousand people—and our funds were limited, but we didn't care if we did nothing more than stroll through Fayette Park and along the old filled-in Erie Canal. Harry's employer, Mr. Ring, had been there with his cousin's family, and he had described all the main sites to see.

It was necessary to take a bus from Wilna Creek, change to a Greyhound bus in Kingston, and cross the St. Lawrence over the recently built Thousand Islands Bridge, which we had only read about. The Dixons drove us to the bus terminal, and we were on our way. We held hands on the bus and by the time we crossed the long span of steel that joined the two countries, it was late afternoon. I stared down at shadows on the surface of the great river and silently repeated my new name, *Georgina Danforth Witley*. I saw not another person on that crowded bus, nor would I ever recall a face from that journey. I was suspended over dark waters that flowed to the sea. I dared to think, *We love each other. We are safe from waves that will batter and strike, but will never break through.* I rested my head on Harry's shoulder. *This is what Grand Dan felt for my grandfather; this is what Phil must have felt for Mr. Holmes—before he began to shout. This is what I see on Ally's face when she exchanges a fast smile with Trick, or when a hand touches his arm as he passes.* I felt heat from Harry's shoulder; I was aware of his thigh pressed against mine. And there was the matter of Grand Dan's long-ago explanation of complementary body parts.

Harry slept the entire way. His hand was warm in mine and I did not try to wake him. I was sorry he'd missed the bridge, but I knew he would see it on the way home. We were wearing matching gold bands, which Harry had purchased by making deposits to Cornelius Ring for the better part of a year.

As the bus approached the terminal in Syracuse, I spotted our hotel from a side street before the driver pulled in to discharge the passengers. The hotel was a walk up the side street and then one long city block and part of another. I shook Harry and he woke, reluctantly. We got off, collected our suitcases and made our way to a busy, divided street with heavy traffic. I had never seen so many cars, and most of them were new. As soon as we checked in and took the elevator upstairs, Harry stretched out on the bed and fell asleep.

Was this supposed to happen? We were alone in a bedroom for the first time; we were married. I sat beside him on the edge of the bed while lights came on in the street below. I tried to wake him, but he shook me off. His voice was harsh. "Let me rest, Georgie," he said. "Leave me alone. I'll get up in a minute."

But he did not.

Two hours later, I was hungry and angry. I had changed my clothes and brushed my hair and moved over to the armchair by the window. I looked out at the lights of the city and stared down at a group of black Americans who were walking by on the street below. I could hear them talking and laughing softly to one another. I woke Harry again and told him the hotel dining room would soon close and I had to eat. He was still wearing his herringbone suit, rumpled from being slept in, and he stared at me as if he couldn't see my face. Was this the loving man I had chosen to marry? The man who had chosen me? He dragged himself up off the bed.

The waiter, a man in his fifties, wore a white shirt with a black vest and bow tie, no jacket. He was cleaning up for the night and was not happy about us coming late to the empty dining room. I must have looked anxious, because he suddenly capitulated and I could tell that he felt sorry for me. "All right," he said. "You can order steak and potatoes. That's about all the cook has left in the kitchen. There might be a few mushrooms, too."

Grateful for any kindness, I promised that we wouldn't linger over the meal. We had set aside enough money for dinners for three days and I was in charge of the funds, which were in a change purse inside my handbag. Breakfasts were included with the room charge, so I didn't have to worry about those. For lunch, we planned to snack on fruit and sandwiches while we were out sightseeing.

Stained glass in the upper windows of the dining room gave a greenish glow to the room, and I suddenly had the feeling that we had swum to the table and were drifting underwater. The waiter's nose looked as if it had taken a blow straight on and as I watched him I thought *septum, buckled septum*. He glanced over at us several times from the doorway to the kitchen, and rubbed at his cheek. He must have wondered at our youth, our silence. We had not spoken a word to each other since we'd sat down. A low lamp hung over our table and, when the steaks were served, Harry raised his elbow as if to block the waiter's approach. As he did, he struck the lamp, which swung crazily over our heads.

"Hey, take it easy," the waiter shouted, and I saw his body tense for a fight.

I let out my breath and came up for air. "Are you sick, Harry? Is something wrong?"

He looked past me, ignored the waiter, stood up and said to neither of us, "I'm going upstairs to my room." The lamp was still swinging. The voice I loved was gone. I cut a large chunk out of my steak and put it in my mouth and tried to chew quickly, but abandoned the rest of the food. I was afraid to ask if I could bring it with me; I did not want pity from the waiter. He picked up a plate in each hand and shrugged. "Have it your way," he said. "But you could have saved the cook the trouble." I paid for the food and, still chewing, followed Harry to the elevator. Upstairs, he collapsed on top of the bed, leaving no room for me. I slept in my clothes in the armchair, and cried half the night. Harry did not move.

In the morning, he was still sprawled on the bedspread, the front of his shirt blotched with perspiration. I wondered if he had become criminally insane. I tried to imagine what my family would say, what they would do in my place. I needed the women around me, Ally and Phil and Grand Dan and Aunt Fred, and I conjured their outrage on my behalf. Oh yes, this was love. This was what they knew. I went into the tiled bathroom and threw up. I had a shower, put on a fresh skirt and blouse and went down to the main floor for breakfast. I ate alone and went back upstairs, fortified. Harry was still asleep. I stood by the bed and forced him to wake. He glared up at me and said, "Who are you?"

Nothing had prepared me for marriage.

I looked at him again and saw that I was staring into darkness. I was so frightened by this, I fought back rage and tears and told myself I'd been denying reality. My husband loved me. He must be sick, out of his mind. I touched his forehead and felt his burning skin.

My first thought was that he would die outside our own country. My second thought was that there was no money in my purse for doctors. Hadn't we been warned that health care was expensive south of the border?

I had to get him home.

I was trembling, and thought my leg bones would not hold me up. I asked Harry if he wanted water, got him to take a few sips, and he lay back down. His eyes stared through me. I went downstairs, paid the bill and told the desk clerk we'd had a change of plans. My body was shaking so much, I had difficulty pressing the elevator buttons. I went back up and found Harry asleep again. I closed my suitcase and lifted his, still locked. I stood at the window, stared down at the median in the busy road below, and calculated the shortest way back to the bus terminal. If I could get Harry across the road directly in front of the hotel, the distance would be shorter than walking all the way to the traffic light and then across. After that, we would have to make our way down the side street.

I had no idea how often buses left for Kingston. I told myself, *You are a big girl, Georgie. You can do this by yourself. You have to get him home.* I threw the strap of my handbag over my shoulder, hauled Harry up and off the bed and made him lean against me. He was still wearing his herringbone suit. I told him to move his feet, to shuffle, to keep himself upright. I picked up my suitcase with my left hand, linked my right arm through his and supported his weight against my side. I took charge. My right hand carried his bumping suitcase between us.

When we reached the elevator, I straightened my spine and thought, *Vertebrae, vertebrae, hold me up*. I had a quick vision of Hubley the headless skeleton being dragged across the page. A man and woman in the elevator stared at us and looked down at the two suitcases. The man eyed Harry suspiciously and then looked away and turned to his wife. "You know that statue of Columbus in the circle?" he said. "They say Mussolini paid the shipping charges to get it here." He shrugged. "That's what I heard. I'm not saying it's true." At the mention of Mussolini, Harry lifted his head but didn't try to speak. He slumped against me again.

In the lobby, I pushed and shoved him past reception, looked straight ahead and reached the outside door. A thin-faced woman followed us out to the sidewalk. It was obvious that she'd been talking to the desk clerk. "Mrs. Witley," she said, "would you like a doctor to see your husband?"

"He's fine," I said, looking past her. "We are both fine." I moved forward. I had heard but not allowed myself to feel pleasure at the words "Mrs. Witley" spoken aloud.

I was streaming with perspiration and wanted to abandon the luggage, but had made a plan and would stick with it. I pushed Harry out into traffic and got as far as the median, horns honking. I sat him down and he fell over. I pulled his legs up onto the grass. I left the suitcases on the median and hauled him up once more and dragged him across the other half of the road. A man leaned his head out of a car window and shouted, "Are you crazy, lady? Are you trying to get yourself killed?" I kept my head down, kept Harry's feet moving, got him across, pushed him up the curb and around the corner, and finally reached the terminal. I sat him on a bench and he slumped over. I checked the schedule. Miracle of miracles, a Kingston bus had pulled up and was due to leave in twenty minutes. I had to run back out to the main road to collect the suitcases, and dodged cars again, parked our luggage beside the bus and pulled Harry to his feet. The driver was standing outside the bus when I got Harry as far as the steps. "Is this your luggage?" he said. He was eyeing the two bags I'd dragged over. Then, he gestured to Harry. "Is this passenger okay? I'm not so sure he should be getting on my bus."

"He's all right. He's tired because we were out late," I said. I feigned a laugh and wondered if it had come out as a scream. I got Harry on board and pushed him to the back of the bus. We sat in a double seat and I believe, after that, he was semi-comatose all the way home. Throughout the trip, the driver stared angrily at me in the mirror. My biggest fear was that we would never get back to our country. I could not allow myself to think that my husband would die on a bus. We recrossed the great river and finally reached Kingston. I dragged Harry off, but the driver was off first and waiting for us.

"Where do you think you're going now?" he said. He was ready for an argument.

"We have to catch a bus to Wilna Creek." I heard my voice, imperious. To myself I said, *And you're not going to stop us.* In eighteen hours, I had become fierce.

He waited until the Wilna Creek bus drove up, and went

over to talk to the other driver. I glared at the two as they con-
ferred, glared as they muttered and shook their heads. We were
permitted to board.

When we reached Wilna Creek, I half-carried Harry down
the steps, and collected our bags. He collapsed to the ground
just as the bus drove away. Although he didn't know who I
was, he seemed to know that we were back, we were home. He
lay on the grass beside the terminal and closed his eyes. I ran
inside to phone the hospital. Within ten minutes, he was being
wheeled on a stretcher through the emergency room doors. I
phoned Ally and she was with me when I received the news,
less than a half hour later.

Harry had polio.

"Your husband is seriously ill," the doctor said. He was angry,
and spoke as if I were a bad child who had caused the illness.
"Where have you been? Where has he come from? Why did you
wait so long to have him admitted?"

So long? This had happened in just over twenty-four hours.
I did not even attempt to explain.

Thus began our marriage. Harry was kept on the Isolation
Ward for three and a half months and, during that time, I was
not permitted to visit. His room was on the ground floor at
the back of the hospital. At the end of the second month of
his illness, he was strong enough to be lifted into a chair by
the window. I had discovered that I could go around and stand
on a grassy patch outside his room and talk to him across the
windowpane. I could barely see inside his room, which was
dimly lit and always in shadow. Much of the time, the windows
were specked with dirt; other days, they were newly washed and
I could clearly see his face. He had lost weight. His shoulders
were thin. Sometimes the blind was up, sometimes down.

When I was alone, I could not get the worry of Mr. Roosevelt out of my mind. He'd died the same year as my father but, years before that, polio had paralyzed his legs. I'd heard talk of *infantile paralysis* when I was a child, and about Mr. Roosevelt's March of Dimes. Would Harry be able to walk when he was permitted to leave the hospital?

The ward staff knew about me standing at the back of the building after work, and no one tried to stop me. Every two or three weeks, I went inside and ventured down the hall as far as the nurses' station to ask about his progress. But in the late afternoon, I was at my post outside the window again. If it rained, I stood under an umbrella.

Harry and I stared at each other across the pane and I told him the story of our wedding. I recounted the bus trip to Syracuse and our wedding night when he slept in his suit. I described the Thousand Islands Bridge, which I had seen twice and he had not seen at all. I told him about the stained-glass windows in the dining room of the hotel, about the waiter's black vest and his buckled nose, and the disbelief on his face when we got up and left two full plates of food. I told him it still made me hungry to think of my uneaten steak. I told him how I'd chewed and chewed that huge mouthful in the elevator and how good it had tasted. I told him he had lain on the grass beside Wilna Creek's bus terminal, and I saw a quiver in his face. I stood outside the window that divided us, and told him I was his wife and that I loved him. If he answered, I did not hear his voice.

Some days, Ally came and stood beside me on the patch of grass, her arm linked through mine. She was pregnant with her daughter, Kathleen, and her belly stuck out so wantonly, she carried a folded raincoat in front of her whenever she left her apartment. If the town thought we were the two demented sisters, we didn't care.

Much of the time, though, I was alone. I looked through the partitioning window and remembered the way Harry had stared at me the morning after we were married.

"Who are you?"

I tried not to believe that I had married a stranger.

TWENTY-FOUR

And that, Lilibet, is the real story of my marriage. Can I help it if the celebration part was short-lived? Is it my fault that sorrow lurks around every corner?

Mr. Ring had already heard the news of Harry's polio. There were two other cases in town, diagnosed before we returned from Syracuse. Everyone knew who they were. When I went to see him, he promised that Harry could return to the jewellery store when he was better. "Your husband is the learner by nature, Mrs. Witley," he said. "Also, he has the eye for design, for intricate work, and I will welcome him back. But only when he is better. Mrs. Ring and I will manage until then." He took my left hand, eyed the wedding ring, nodded approvingly and patted me on the shoulder.

Ira had given me a week off for my honeymoon. As Harry and I had already paid a month's rent, I moved into our rented house alone so that I could be close to both store and hospital. I had only my own salary, but told myself that I would find a way to manage. Part of me was afraid. I'd never lived by myself before; I wasn't used to the noises of the house, the fall winds blowing through the eaves. At night, I pulled the covers over my head and tried to block the sound. In the daytime, I was fine. The house wasn't that far from Ally and Trick's place, and I saw them frequently. They were in the upstairs apartment of a house only two streets away.

When I returned to work, part of my job, as well as helping customers and ordering supplies, was to restock counters and displays. To get a few moments to myself, I sometimes went downstairs and walked between ceiling-high shelves in the stockroom, a windowless basement room where I stared up at rows of look-alike boxes, trying to familiarize myself with new products Ira kept adding to the stock. I tugged edges of torn brown paper over fabric ends to protect them from dust. I daydreamed down there, and thought about the husband I was not permitted to visit. I wondered about my future, which had shrunk from being an open space stretching before me, and had turned into a bottomless pit. I was still going round to the back of the hospital every day after work, and I was still concerned about the lasting effects of the disease on Harry's health.

After what I now thought of as my "polio honeymoon," I'd begun to notice that Ira had a new way of looking at me that I did not like. One day, he followed me down to the stockroom. I had my back to him and did not hear him on the stairs. He came up behind me and placed both hands on my waist and squeezed, sliding his hands upward. I let out a yelp and whipped around, elbowing him sharply in the ribs. I could see individual bristles on his cheeks. Because of his shape, he had curled around me like a spoon. I startled myself and him, and we both pulled back in surprise. He cursed and, holding his side, climbed back up the stairs and never sneaked up on me again. Even so, the feel of his ribs was stuck to my elbow and, for the rest of the day, I had the sensation that something rotten was attached to my skin.

After that, I stopped daydreaming in the stockroom, and kept Ira at a distance. But I often stared at his receding mandible and remembered Miss Grinfeld's warnings in our one-room school about the connection between chinless families and bad behaviour. I regretted that I had not foreseen the danger.

Harry was discharged from hospital November 20, 1947, the day Elizabeth married her handsome Philip of Greece, who was slender, like Harry, and rumoured to have been born on a tabletop in Corfu, which was not easy to imagine. Philip was a distant cousin to Elizabeth, also descended from Victoria, their great-great, as most of Europe's Royal Houses seemed to be. I read every magazine and newspaper I could find, every detail of the forthcoming marriage, the family tree, the expected guests.

I believed the coincidence of dates—Harry's discharge and the Royal Wedding—to be a positive sign. I thought of Harry collapsing to the grass, and was reminded of the small boy who'd had stick legs and was carried around on an English pillow. I understood that Harry's bones had been too weak to hold him up as a child, and I was forced to abandon, for all time, my fantasy picture of *satin, tassels, prince*.

All week, I'd been watching the stores in town tack up bunting and streamers in display windows. Ira ordered a huge, rectangular cake iced in the colours of the flag, and it was my job when the doors opened on Royal Wedding Day to serve one slice each to the first hundred customers who walked into the store. It seemed that everyone in the County had come to town; the sales from that single day were the largest ever recorded in the ledgers. I thought Mr. Holmes would have approved, and wished he'd thought of something similar when he'd been running things during the Depression.

Lilibet's ring was made from a nugget of Welsh gold, and she was bedecked with seed pearls and flowers. The silk in her veil came from Chinese silkworms, thousands of spinning caterpillars fulfilling their destinies. When I saw pictures of her gown and veil later, I threw away my pork-pie hat. After I served the flag cake to the lineup of customers—which included Phil, Grand Dan, and Ally, who pushed Kathleen in her brand new carriage—and after I'd stood at the cash register ringing in sales, Ira, flushed with his own success, permitted me to leave early.

I walked to the hospital, collected Harry, and we took a taxi directly to our house, which I had done my best to fix up. Because it was a bungalow, there were no stairs for Harry to negotiate, not even cellar stairs. His body had been weakened, but the doctor said he could return to work. He was not crippled, but the muscles of his left leg had atrophied, and he limped, a small price to pay. That night, for the first time, we slept in each other's arms in the same bed. Our parts were complementary. I understood that at a time of reunion, there is nothing important to say until all the loving is out of the way.

Sternum

TWENTY-FIVE

Harry remembered nothing of the trip except boarding the bus in his wedding suit after the Dixons drove us to the terminal. For a while, he joked that he'd never been to the States, but I was not amused. He remembered one other detail, and that was the flower I wore with my blue suit. He was right about that; Grand Dan snipped a yellow rose from her wagon-wheel garden before we left the Danforth house for the church. She pinned it to my lapel with two tiny gold safety pins taken from the emergency heap that was still on the windowsill beside the back door.

Now, my right eye is clouding. Dark spots dart in and out and around, and that is a worry. I've made progress; I've inched along. But when I move, the car moves, too. Or does it only seem that way because night is closing in? How many nights? I have no way of knowing.

Nothing is certain, Lilibet, though I wish you would rally your faithful guards and send them out to search for me. Have I dreamed my life, invented it as I lie here? Have I invented

you? Now that I'm away from it, I see that the half-dead tree
leans more heavily than I first thought. It could fall in the forest, but surely not without warning. This old monument will
groan and stretch and yawn and cry before it topples. But my
eye gives me grief; black spots swim before me; part of me runs
ragged-edged into panic. I need my eyes; I need my vision. *Let
me not go out in darkness, Lord.*

In high school, I was required to learn the cranial nerves for
biology, and I went home to check out *Gray's*. Olfactory, Optic,
Oculomotor . . . Of the twelve, Optic is the one whose diagram I know best. The eyeball, a round balloon, drifted up the
height of the page, a single disc-like blip on its surface. It rose
to the right and lifted off a two-pronged stem, like ice held by
a pair of tongs. *On Old Olympus Tiny Tops, A Finn And German
Viewed Some Hops.*

The devices of learning. Do they never leave the brain?
Maybe they're the last to go.

Despondency presses on my soul. I have to fight it off. It's
humiliating to lie here like this, to be helpless.

There's always God to lift the spirits.

Did He listen before, when my spirits were down? Was He
there to hear?

Is this the time for greater questions?

Maybe it is. I have all the time in the world.

Time might be running out.

Well God might be there, and He might not. The truth of
the matter is I used to welcome the hope of having a faith as
strong as Grand Dan's.

Doubts crept in?

Not when I was a child, but after that. When loss was too
great to ponder. I turned away.

Don't depress yourself, Georgie.

I'll sing. Singing lifts my spirits. I'll sing to God, whether He's there or not—just in case. I still know all the hymns.

Belt one out, then.

Ezekiel saw two wheels a'rollin
Way in the middle of the air
Ezekiel saw two wheels a'rollin
Way in the middle of the air
Oh, the big wheel ran by steam
And the little wheel ran by the grace of God
Ezekiel saw two wheels a'rollin
Way in the middle of the air

I learned that in school. And now I know that it requires more spit than "Onward Christian Soldiers." Some hymns are drier than others.

Thirst, oh thirst. The body craves.

"Water," said Miss Grinfeld, "is the necessity of life," and commanded us to create a poster of its sources, on a Friday afternoon.

I thought of Uncle Fred, and drew a pump.

Pure water, pure air, pure joy, pure hope. Youth promises hope. The word *future* portends hope.

But I'm dying.

Don't talk nonsense.

I've lived my life and that's that. And what was the point of it? What have I done? Has anyone paid attention? I'm from a time that is dismissed, deemed unimportant. Women my age are invisible. When we reach our sixties, we're discounted, sidelined. Even before that. But it's our world, too. We live in it and we are many. I've lived in it every day for eighty years.

You're ranting like a defeatist.

Sometimes I feel as if I'm still the child walking on crusted snow with arms outstretched, hoping with each step that I won't break through. But for some time now, people have looked through me. When Case directed *Death of a Salesman* and the salesman's wife declared from the stage that attention must be paid, I wanted to stand up and shout agreement.

I can already hear the voices when my body is found: "It was a blessing, really."

For heaven's sake, Georgie, get a grip.

That's the way I feel. It happens sometimes, and that's the truth. Highs and lows. I'm in a low.

You've pulled out of low points before.

Nadirs. But I've never been this far down. If only the mind would rest. At least I finished *War and Peace*.

If the mind rests, you're dead. It's that cut and dried.

That was blunt enough. But what have I ever done to merit attention being paid?

Pick up a thread. Think of other things.

New life gives hope. Did Lilibet and her Duke laugh aloud when little Charles was born? A Royal Salute marked the event in Ottawa in November '48, and I imagined I could hear the guns more than a hundred miles away. One month later, Case was born and, like the biblical Sarah, I laughed for joy to see her. Her eyes were puffy, her ears flattened, her fingers long and slender like Harry's, her feet blue. One side of her lip curled upward in a smile. She was so tiny, she fit between elbow and palm along the inside of Harry's arm. He could scarcely believe he could hold her in one hand. Her tininess didn't last; she ended up as long-legged as Grand Dan, taller than I am—or was, before I began to shrink. She also inherited Grand Dan's hair; a black mop of it reached down almost to her eyebrows. I was awed, overawed. For weeks, I managed to convince myself that I was the only mother in the world. From the moment Case took her first breath, she and I became something new, something never before known.

And so began the raising of my daughter, the child who had to have the last word, the last sound, the last *hmmph* through her teeth, the last noisy huff blown through her nostrils while she trotted to her room—where she was sometimes sent.

Did it harm anything? She got the last word. I didn't worry.

I had stopped working for Ira, but my days were full. And I so loved my child, I was not at all put out to learn, when she was two, that I was pregnant again. "We have room in our hearts," I told her confident little self. "We have plenty of love left over for the baby who's coming."

And so we did, the three of us, when our son was born. I had to stay in hospital for a week before I was allowed to bring him home, and that is when Case first met him. We named him Matthias, after my grandfather, and Grand Dan held him at his christening. Unlike the rest of the family, unlike any of us, his hair was blond and his skin fair. Harry, with no memory of his parents, did not know who our son resembled.

What went wrong? There is always buzzing, humming in my head when I re-enter the baby's room in the late afternoon, for I have entered it behind my eyes a thousand thousand times. It was late fall and there had been an unusually early but light snowfall. Case had been taken to Ally's to play outside with her cousin, Kathleen, for the afternoon. It was chilly in the house and I had wrapped Matt in a soft blanket before putting him down for his nap. He was five months and two days old. His eyes were large and round and when he looked up at me before I laid him in the crib, he smiled as if a joke had passed between us. He had a perfect little body and I hugged him close and hummed into the folds of his neck. I planted a kiss on his cheek and tucked him on his side, with a bolster behind his back. He slept longer than usual, so I went into the darkened room to wake him before Harry came home and before Case was dropped off by Ally. It was the time of blue light, just before dusk—my favourite part of the afternoon. I raised the blind carefully so I wouldn't startle the baby, and went to stand beside his crib. There was complete silence. I did not put on the light. The blanket was close to his face, and I pulled it back. I touched his shoulder and my arm seized as if it were paralyzed. I knew the instant I touched him that something was wrong. There was no slight stirring, no baby yawn, no groggy smile as he woke. I turned him onto his back and picked him up and held him close so that I could see his face. His eyes did not open. His beautiful skin was cold. His precious life gone. He had been dead for some time, I don't know how long. There had been no sound. I had been close by, all afternoon.

Did I wrap him too tightly? Did he pull in his little sternum, trying to get air? Was the blanket too close to his face? Did he smother? Did I smother my own child? Am I responsible for my beloved baby's death?

I sank to the floor, to the braided rug we had laid on the floorboards beside his crib. I wrapped myself around my son. I tried to breathe life back into him. When I knew I had to give up, I stayed there on the floor, and pressed his cold and perfect body into mine. I tried to warm him. And that is how Harry found us, in the dark.

It is terrible to be alone here, in the dark. I can't pretend it is not. I am getting colder and colder, though I continue to move my arm, my leg, drag myself a little, even in the night. The aloneness makes the space around me unfillable, vast.

I would like to sleep.

I have never stopped, *can* never stop asking why. Why give my baby life only to take it away? I can't stop asking because I have thought of him every day since that day, every day of my life. I came to understand that I could not get through even one day without pictures flashing through memory: his fair skin, the light in his hair, his trusting baby self, his fat tummy jiggling in the bathwater, his eyes exchanging a joke with me. I understood—but it took a long time to gain this knowledge— that in order to get through any day, rather than fighting off the images I held in my head, it was better to set aside a time each morning to remember. It did not take away the despair or the anger, the loss or the guilt. It did not take away the love. But it helped me to get out of bed in the morning.

Where did hope go? It was swallowed by a dark pit that I had not seen lurking.

I had my family. I had Grand Dan, Ally, Trick, Phil, Aunt and Uncle Fred, all of whom rallied around. Harry, like me, was angry. We could not understand; we never did. And we had Case, whose life had to carry on in the midst of grief, and who became more precious to us both.

We buried our baby in the cemetery in the Danforth plot. The service was held in our country church. Once more, I sat in the front pew with my family and held hands. This time, Harry was beside me.

After the funeral, I returned home and thought of our baby being smothered a second time by the weight of dirt heaped upon his tiny coffin. I couldn't bear the image. I walked into the living room, picked up the tree of life that had belonged to my grandfather and threw it against the wall. It shattered, the glass leaves strewn, the slender branches hanging from threads of frayed silk. That night, Harry and I clung to each other in our bed and wept.

There has never been such grief.

TWENTY-SIX

I received no help from God. There was no one to rail against. If there had been someone to blame, I'd have demanded an explanation, if only to loosen the tightness around my heart.

I knew that Phil had loved the baby and was grieving too, but the adage of her generation was: *Set your jaw, grit your teeth, take one day at a time. This is what life hands you and you have to bear up.* None of this would have helped. She sensed this, and held her tongue. When I saw her, it was all I could do to keep from pulling her grief on top of my own.

I knew, too, that many soldiers had not come back from the war, that other women were mourning husbands and fathers, brothers and sons. Their grief was not connected to mine. I pushed the sorrow deep inside and tried to bury it.

Grand Dan began to come to town. She arranged for someone to drive her—Trick, or someone from a neighbouring farm. She appeared at my door, came in and sat in the kitchen or living room, doing needlework or reading, or playing softly with Case. I never knew which days she would arrive. We did not have to talk about the baby; his name was always there, between us. It was her presence that mattered. Her quiet, soothing presence. When Harry came home from work, he drove her back to the country. This went on for weeks.

I threw my energies into raising Case.

Case was not a joiner, and I was glad she had her cousin, Kathleen, to play with. As she grew older, she refused group activities except for Sunday School, which she liked because the teacher took the class on nature hikes and told stories while they walked. Case loved to read, loved language and tried it every which way. She'd been born with theatre in her blood, and she dictated dialogue for me to write down when she was three and four and five. After that, she printed the lines on her own. I was sorry Miss Grinfeld had retired and moved away, because she'd have liked my daughter. But the one-room school was closed and, anyway, we lived in town. By then I was old enough to understand that I had loved Miss Grinfeld when I was a child.

Case invented plays and held "dress reversals." Her stage successes were her "bictories." She made sets from tarpaper and tin outside, and dragged branches into the house to create a forest inside. She hung old drapes over chair-backs and popped her head through, experimenting with voice. If I turned on the radio while she was inventing, she told me, "Music subtracts me, Momma, when I'm trying to concentrate." One day, I heard her creating a dialogue for babies in heaven. I stood in the middle of the room and could not move. She stopped what she was doing and said, "Momma, did baby Matt's bones stay connected when he was buried in the grave? Did they go up to the sky when he went to heaven? Did they?"

I turned my back and walked to the table and sat there and

cried without sound. She climbed to my lap and wiped my cheeks with her small palms. She climbed down again and went back to her play.

The more she became involved in theatrical games, the more I helped. I tried to create costumes—I was good at making flawless tinfoil tiaras—but anything I sewed on the new machine was a disaster. Phil and Grand Dan came to the rescue. Much later, when Case was in her teens, she began to talk about "the imaginative beyond." I looked at her strangely. I helped her to learn parts for school plays, and we sat on kitchen chairs facing each other and read corresponding roles. Her explorations into imagination made mine seem impoverished. But I understood her spirit. It was the underground connection between us.

Every once in a while, I walked to the tobacco store to peruse the lineup of current magazines. I cashed the family allowance and occasionally allotted a tiny portion for news of Lilibet and her growing family. When he grew out of rompers, Charles wore button-up coats over short pants and bare legs. The Queen wore comfortable frocks when she looked out for her bonny son—though I wondered how much unseen help was hidden in the background. She also wore a diamond brooch with her frocks, sometimes pearls, which I never wore when I was caring for Case, even though Harry presented me with a double strand for Christmas—dubbed "Lizzie's pearls" because they were similar in design to the ones in the photos.

Charles grinned with an impish smile and stared unblinking into the camera. When he was amused, he cried out in delight, or so it was reported. Anne arrived, and sat up in her pram with blonde hair and raspberry-tinted lips that appeared to be lipsticked on the glossy pages. I wondered if Lilibet understood that she was blessed. In family photos, Philip stood to one side, slightly aloof. There was always a corgi, on leash or off, depending.

And there was the Queen—*Majesty, Mother of two*—into whose hems hidden weights were sewn to defeat any gust of wind that came along and tried to lift her skirt. She carried handbags that slipped up over her arm so she'd be free to shake hands. Not unlike the women of Wilna Creek, she wore gloves out of doors. Every woman in town—this included Ally and me—had gloves in a top drawer, a black pair and a white. We wore gloves to the A&P to shop for groceries, which, from the bottom of a ravine, is hard to believe.

Our fathers were dead, and Lilibet was Queen. In every one of those magazines, she had a smile on her face. If not a smile, a square-shouldered look into the far-off future, as if what we were all facing was bright and promising indeed. What *she* was facing was the birth of more children and a shrinking pink map. The Empire on which the sun never set was changing quickly. But give credit where credit is due. Lilibet had a job and she held her head high. Lilibet led with her chin.

TWENTY-SEVEN

Thousands of new people were arriving in our country, and Wilna Creek had begun to stretch its boundaries. In the stores, in the library, everywhere I went, I heard conversations about "the influx of DPs." Case's classmates had names like Bep and Wilhelmina and Rom. From all sides, women were told to get back into their homes after the war, and stay there. I was home, making every penny stretch. Ally was home, drawing and painting at one end of her kitchen. She had a bursting portfolio labelled "WHITE" in her hall closet, but still had not displayed a single piece of art. She and I had a child-swap arrangement, which suited us both. I volunteered at the school and the town library. Every second Sunday, both families drove to the country to have Sunday supper with Phil and Grand Dan. Before Case was born, Harry had bought a second-hand Hudson, and I had learned to drive.

What astonishes me now is that every hour was filled to overflowing and yet, looking back at that intense period, all the days seem like one day. I wondered more than once if I had become frantic about filling them up. I read to Case and acted out roles and helped her build theatre sets and volunteered and washed and ironed and painted walls and gardened and put up preserves and gave birthday parties and made radish roses and fancy sandwiches—checkerboards, wagon wheels, pinwheels—stuck a gherkin in the centre and added a crabapple for garnish. Ally and I visited back and forth and looked after our children and went to see our mother and grandmother and hosted Christmas and Thanksgiving celebrations, ensuring that if Aunt Fred was visiting she was served only white meat and Phil only dark. Ally and I did our own housework and hated it. And throughout all of this time, each event flew down like a separate pattern threading itself through a bolt of cloth. Each moment hummed with energy, shifted and settled until assured its own space and shape. And then, some unseen hand darted a needle into the entire long bolt and drew it together so that all of the patterns merged and no single image could be unravelled or pried off.

But sometimes I manage to slip a finger of memory inside a fold of those years and expose a seam. One day at the library, I was asked to arrange magazines in the Reading Corner. I flipped through them as I worked, and a magazine fell open to its back pages. I cast my eye over a list of ads under the heading "Men Wanted." Two lines in bold print, placed by "small New York company," invited applicants to submit samples of work for part-time employment as an illustrator for health and biology pamphlets and texts. The work could be done by correspondence.

I copied out the ad, put the information in my purse, and had a sense of expanding possibilities. Didn't I hold the shape of body parts in my head? Didn't I have a man's name? I drafted

a letter and signed it George Witley. I drew a set of lungs with
an inset of popcorn-shaped alveoli. I included larynx, trachea,
tongue, nasal and oral cavities. With dotted lines, I showed the
position of blood vessels and a shadow of the heart, including
the aorta and the superior vena cava. I labelled the diagram
"The Respiratory System" and folded the drawing and placed
it in an envelope with the letter. I carried the envelope around
in my purse. Case became ill the same week, and I sponged her
at night to keep down the fever. She was delirious; her lungs
were congested. She was diagnosed with pneumonia, and I was
terrified. Grand Dan came in from the country to stay, and
sponged her, and made onion plasters and took turns sitting
at the bedside with Harry and me. Harry took time off from
work because he was afraid not to be present. We stumbled
along the hall at night and spelled each other off. The doctor
advised us to care for Case at home but we were told to watch
her carefully. We could not look each other in the eye because
of our fear. When Case began to recover and was able to sit
up, Harry went back to work and Grand Dan returned home.
Case and I looked out her bedroom window and created roles
for a theatre of clouds. Two lambs reared up on their hind feet
and bleated. A lion trapped a mouse under its paw. A cumulus
blew its stack and became a volcano. A cloth doll exploded, its
stuffing scattered over the heavens. A barn roof burned. A dog
chewed at cellar steps. The drawing in my purse was forgotten
and never mailed. Anyway, it was Ally who was the artist in
the family.

TWENTY-EIGHT

Although the damage to Harry's left leg did not permit him to stand for hours, he had steady hands and quickly learned about escape mechanisms and mainsprings, hairsprings and balance wheels. It helped that he had long, slender fingers. He wore magnified lenses while seated at his jeweller's table and sometimes a loupe, which pushed a telltale depression into his skin. He began to design necklaces and brooches, and Mr. Ring assured him that he had a talent for both.

Harry loved Case and me, I was certain of that, but there were times when he pulled into himself. When this first happened, he pulled so far back I saw darkness that left no room for anyone.

At the table, Case, who was lingering too long over her food, asked a question about his childhood. "Were you allowed to leave food on your plate when you were a little boy, Daddy?" Harry appeared to be bewildered by the question, and didn't answer. He did not speak again during the rest of the meal. Later, after I'd put Case to bed and tucked her in, he turned away from me. What was he living through? The early years had left their mark.

Another time, we were visiting Phil and Grand Dan when a summer storm blew up. Harry did not like storms and I wondered how he had survived at sea during the war. He hated thunder and lightning and I believe this also had something to do with his childhood—the cruelty on the farm, being sent alone to sleep in a cold and cheerless shed.

Phil could hear the storm, far off, but she was listening to Mario Lanza. She had discovered him when she and Grand Dan had gone to see *The Great Caruso* at the Belle, and she was telling Case about him while they listened to the one precious recording she owned of Lanza's songs. She loved to do her sewing to his voice and, most times we visited, he was singing in the background.

Grand Dan called us to the window to see the curtain of rain that blocked the sky as a wall of storm approached. Spectacular bolts of lightning were shooting down to earth. Harry waited until the storm was immediately overhead and then, with rain pounding the roof, he went halfway up the stairs and sat on a step in the dark while thunder threatened to crack open the house. It was the kind of storm that could provoke desperate fear or giddy elation. The power went out. Phil lit a kerosene lamp and sat Case on her lap and began to tell her the story of Caruso's life as lived through Mario Lanza.

I went to sit by Harry on the stairs. He could not believe how much I enjoyed watching trees whip back and forth in wind gone wild. Indeed, as children, Ally and I had often stood in the enclosed veranda watching for the quick line of flames that ran along wires strung between poles up the lane. Glass insulators burst and fell to the ground and, after each storm, we went

outside to search for their rounded caps. We brought them to
Grand Dan, who wired them to the side of her chicken coop
and filled them with water. The yellow fluffballs that were baby
chicks ran to them and dipped their tiny beaks, and drank.

At the end of the storm, Harry came down off the stairs and
no one seemed to think his behaviour worthy of mention or
remark. Grand Dan, however, brought him to the parlour later
and talked to him. From the kitchen I could hear her murmur
something about the war.

Harry never tried to explain his behaviour. Nor did he offer
to drive me to the place to which he'd been sent as a Home
Child, so that he could point out the farm from the road. He
must have known where it was. A three-day walk would not
have been so far, measured in a boy's steps. The farm would
probably be considered close—now that most families, including ours, owned a car and took Sunday drives in the country.
But I never learned the name of the abusive family or the place
Harry had been sent to live. Both had been banished from his
conscious mind.

Despite the polio honeymoon that began our marriage,
despite the frightening memories and the darkness that sur-
faced, despite the loss of our son, there came an evening when
love for Harry stamped its indelible image for all time. Case
was reciting one of her own creations at the table while I
was preparing supper, and I was half-listening. Harry usually
walked home from the jewellery store but because it was raining, Mr. Ring had offered him a drive. When the car pulled
up, I glanced through the white sheers at the window, just as
Harry was getting out of the passenger seat. He stood beside
the car and opened the rear door and reached in. I saw his lips
move as he spoke to Mr. Ring. He rounded the hood and I

registered the familiar limp, at the same time noticing that he held something in his right hand. He leaned into the rain, and then straightened. His fingers were wrapped around the stems of a bouquet of yellow roses. He glanced down at the ground and I saw determination and purpose on his face.

I was witnessing an act of love.

Harry had brought flowers to me on other occasions, and he would do so again, but it is this memory that has stayed with me. In one brief moment, all darkness was dispelled.

In the image, there is motion. Harry is rounding the car, preoccupied. He is bearing a gift. The memory would not be the same if I had not looked out at that precise moment. Harry's intent, the courtship ritual, his trim and limping body—these are the details I witnessed. He was returning home after a day's work. His wife and daughter were inside. He was related to two people he could call family. His hands were bearing roses.

I loved him when I married him, but this day I loved him for all time.

Easy as pie.

Who said pie was easy? Phil's pie crust was as heavy as lead, and mine wasn't much better. It was Grand Dan who knew the secret of pie crust.

But knowing the depth of my love at that moment was easy. As pie.

Ribs

TWENTY-NINE

Can I be seen from above? What day is it? Has the Queen's Lunch come and gone? If so, Lilibet has already greeted her guests. Case told me that the ninety-nine names were chosen by ballot so that selection would be fair, so that all parts of the kingdom would be represented.

Lilibet's kingdom. Well, it must be something, having a kingdom.

Case was the first to find out about the celebration, and looked up the information on her computer. How she manages to locate things in that machine is a mystery to me. I've been in her apartment when she sits in front of the monitor and laughs into the screen as if it will respond. "Ha Ha Ha." It makes me wonder about the future of civilization. She wants me to get a computer of my own so that we can communicate by e-mail, but that is preposterous. Why would I do that when we live in the same town? Case, slipping in the last word as always, said, "You'll change your mind, you'll see. If you don't, you'll be left behind. You ought to buy a cellphone, too. You might need it someday."

Cassandra, blessed with the gift of prophecy and never believed. Well, she was right. I'm sorry I didn't buy a cellphone. And for sure I'm not going anywhere. I'm stuck here with painful breaks in my bones, and ribs that have begun to fuse. True ribs, false ribs, floating ribs, peculiar ribs, elastic arches of ribs. When I looked inside *Gray's* I saw a great half-hoop of ribs welcoming the turn of a page.

After he sold the jewellery store and retired—he had bought the business when Mr. Ring died—Harry fractured ribs three summers in a row by falling through rotting canvas seats of lawn chairs he'd neglected to fix. He was good at repairing miniature things, but not items that were bulky or large. We were living up the hill by then. A stack of canvas chairs had been left behind by the previous owners and were leaning into the garage wall. As the canvas rotted, so did Harry fall through. I heard the sickening, telltale snap at the instant of the spill from the sling seat, just before he rolled to the ground. He planned to replace the canvas with wooden slats in all of the chairs, but didn't get around to doing the repairs. After being treated for the first fracture, he refused to return to hospital to be X-rayed. He already knew the diagnosis, he said.

He had a stubborn streak, and so did I. Every summer, I looked to the sky, rolled my eyes and gave a nod to Grandfather Danforth's third principle while Harry lay on the ground, unwilling to either learn or change his behaviour. Turning down my offer of assistance, he managed to pick himself up and go inside. To counteract the pain, understood to be an ordinary tribulation of summer, he borrowed a stretched and loose girdle from my dresser drawer, stepped into it and pulled it up over his chest. He told me he was strapping his ribs. The girdle was one of those old flesh-coloured items we women had to wear when we lived in the dark ages and were not meant to breathe. I had no use for it, but had not thrown it away. After Harry's first fracture, I kept it for the dog days of summer.

Structure determines function. Life does come down to its basics.

I hear cars again. The world is going on without me. I have to punch air, kick my leg, ward off clots. I miss solving my crossword in the morning. I miss eating a tuna sandwich while standing at the kitchen counter. I never stood for meals until after Harry died, and now I rarely sit. I miss hearing the news, flicking the switch on my radio, the dial set to CBC. I miss having a bath. I miss my ordinary day.

The best walks Harry and I had were in the fall when the trees in the ravine burst into glorious blaze. I often wished I had learned to play the trumpet so that I could stand beneath the showiest tree and blow my horn on its behalf. I think of Satchmo, out of breath. Or Buddy Bolden on his cornet. Or Jelly Roll Morton, wheeling a piano down the root-strewn path playing "Jelly Roll Blues." I think of Rice strumming his guitar on Case's summer stage, soft and easy, a sound that makes you want to curl up under a canopy of branches.

I miss jazz at suppertime. I miss the way I settle in to close each day. Rice told me my radio doesn't have good sound, but to my ears it's fine. Anyway, I have a CD player in my bedroom, compliments of Case. But the kitchen is where I spend my time; my radio connects me, assures that I'm one with my country. It isn't until nighttime that I begin to have doubts.

I don't watch television because TV images are frightening, damaging, terror-laden. They make people take sides, one extreme or another. After 9/11, I watched TV day and night until I could take no more. Harry couldn't pry me away from the screen. I wanted to understand but could not. I sat on the chesterfield and on the third day began to cry and thought I would never stop. Harry turned off the TV and brought me my jacket and we walked out the back door in silence, and down a steep trail into the ravine. We passed this very spot. A terrible thing had happened and the new world was carrying on. A couple of years later, Saddam's sons, Uday and Qusay, were killed in Iraq in a shootout and, a day after that, the stock market in New York began to revive. Who pretends to understand? To think that Grandfather gave his life to one war and Harry was wounded in the next, and each prayed that his war would be the last.

I just realized that on Wednesday, the 19th of April, the day of the Birthday Lunch—whether it's come or gone—the Queen will be the only person in the whole world who will know that I am missing.

THIRTY

I have a narrow view of heaven from here, a V-shaped opening between trees. A wisp of cloud drifts past, a mouth with open lips spewing smoke. If I squint to block the trees, I hang from the wisp of cloud, drift on the thread of smoke.

I regret to say that I began to smoke—a cigarette here and there, nothing serious or deadly—during the months that followed Harry's death. I had begun to find things. I drove down the hill and bought a pack of Benson & Hedges at one of those ugly strip malls that have sprung up around the edge of town. I lit the first while standing at the kitchen window and blew smoke out through the screen, not wanting to rebreathe it later. I can still bring back the floating sensation after the first pull into the lungs, the dizziness, the body sensing that it is off-kilter. I stowed the cigarettes in the freezer, in case I needed further propping up.

I found unexpected things.

Strands of black wool that had fallen from the fringes of Grand Dan's shawl, which I inherited after her death. The more I wore the shawl, the more the fringe fell from its edges. I left the pieces where they dropped because I loved the idea of moving about the planet and dispersing something created by Grand Dan. Separately and individually, each strand might have resembled a three-inch black worm but, for me, each was a deposition of love. During the Big Trip, I tightened the shawl around my shoulders while I stood on a battlefield at the Somme and honoured a grandfather I'd never met. I shredded the War Office telegram Grand Dan had received in 1916 and scattered its bloodstained pieces in a farmer's field. The next day, I wrapped the shawl around me at Vimy Ridge and traced my grandfather's carved name with my fingertips while I cried for all of us. I wore it in Austria, Switzerland, Italy, Cyprus and Greece. It sheltered me in airplanes, airports, taxicabs, trams and, one hot summer later, on a ferry in Seattle. Wherever I travelled, I left bits of Grand Dan behind.

But after Harry died, I discovered a soft, wormy nest of those same pieces in the bottom drawer of a desk in his basement workroom. As the wool had fallen, so had Harry followed and gathered it up. I felt betrayed. I wanted those bits of Grand Dan and the stains of her blood to be left on black earth that had roiled over the shattered pieces of my grandfather's body. I wanted them left on a bench worn smooth in a foreign metro, or stuck to a fence surrounding a dogs' park in Geneva, or snagged on the slit seat of a Roman bus, or caught in slivers of boardwalk beside the Ligurian Sea. A bird with yellow wings might have flown off with a strand to line a nest. A Greek gardener with leathery hands might have used one to tie a tomato plant, or to support an olive branch. But Harry had followed me, and thwarted these acts of my imagination.

This should not have surprised me. He once tracked me on a crowded beach after I went for a walk. He could identify my footprints in the sand. If he were alive today and knew I was missing, he'd find me in a minute. He was expert at observing the smallest detail; it was as if his eyes had begun to magnify without the loupe. When *I* looked for messages in the sand, all I could see were cross-hatches of heel and toe prints. How could anyone separate one set of tracks from an entire human medley?

Harry could. Harry was a tracker.

He was also a hoarder.

Other items found after his death: a soft-sided black diary, palm-sized, which he had kept when he was single during the thirties, after he'd left the Dixon farm and moved to town. The diary listed every job he worked at before joining up. I read and reread the entries, and tried to understand the young man Harry had been before he entered my life. The first entries were from 1936 and included items such as these:

— *Three days work at canning factory.*
— *Blizzards all week. Attended sleigh-riding party.*
— *Dominion Day, hiked to river to attend church picnic. Long walk there, ride back to town in Ford car.*
— *Threshed grain for one dollar and two meals per day.*
— *Employed by CNR shovelling coal and lining track on coal dump, 25 cents per hour.*

I looked for clues. There was not a single emotional detail, only a chronicling of events that had to do with staying alive during the final years of the Depression.

Another item: a Metropolitan Life Insurance booklet with an illustration of a child carrying a chair: *When I go walking with my chair / I hold it high up in the air.*

When Case was four, Harry helped her to read the Met. Life booklets, sent to us in the mail. One booklet had illustrations of carrots, an apple, white bread and a chicken leg. Case loved it. Harry also taught her to recognize the countries of the world on a large map that hung on our kitchen wall. I have not yet come across the map.

More findings.

Inside a narrow box, a row of discarded boots, paired as if a bevy of feet might someday arrive to slip them on.

Six heels from old shoes, stuffed into a plastic container with a lid.

A canister labelled "Things that tie." Inside were neatly rolled pouches of string, tangles of used shoelaces, and yellow skatelaces flecked with black.

Pantyhose legs cut into strips for tying runner beans.

Paper bags filled with seeds.

Paper bags filled with pods.

A cigar box packed with rotted elastic bands. These lifted out as one solid piece and gave off a rancid odour.

A second cigar box filled with green tie tapes stored in clusters of ten, with an eleventh tape bound around the middle of each cluster. I threw them out immediately and tried not to dwell on this discovery. Each middle tie represented a mean little twist, and I wondered at which point in his life Harry had saved them.

It was as if he had stored these items against an expected day when his belongings would be stolen or forcefully taken from him. I thought of the times he'd been sorrowful and moody. I thought of him making deliberate moves to protect his hidden goods, all labelled and secreted away. I raised my head and spoke to Lilibet in the thinning air. "Do you think it's possible that I married my father?"

I began to worry about what else I would find. I told myself that Harry had been a Home Child; he'd lived in a shed throughout his childhood; he'd owned nothing, not even a pair of laces. Were these the hoardings of the same man who, one evening after work, stood outside and, seeing me at the window holding up our toddler, jumped into the air and clicked his heels? The leap lasted only a moment, but what a sight! Case clapped her hands and called for more.

Harry, I hardly knew ye.

THIRTY-ONE

There was more.

A cache of photos hidden beneath the hinged lid of Harry's bedside table. It took a while to get to this discovery, because a brass lamp sat on top of the table, undisturbed. After Harry's death, it was a long time before I looked inside.

He must have waited until I was out of the house to inspect or add to his cache. He'd have had to lift the lamp, place it on the floor, have enough time to get the photos out and back in again. He chose his hiding place well, because I found the photos only months after his death. I was thinking of donating the table to the Sally Ann, removed the lamp, raised the lid and there was Harry's version of family, inside. I spent the rest of the afternoon in our room, trying to recreate an order he might have seen. It was a celebration of the people he loved.

This is my understanding, my glimpse of family seen through Harry's eyes.

At the top of the heap was his first family, the brother and sister who had been lost to him when he was a boy. Verna and

Gordo had also been Home Children, and had tried to trace Harry's whereabouts for more than half a century. They finally found him—found us—on a snowy night one Canadian winter. Unannounced, the two of them and Verna's husband, Arman, walked through our front door on the seventh of December, the night of Harry's sixty-fifth birthday. It was the same year Harry and I took our Big Trip.

The tracker had been tracked.

Until the knock on the door, Harry had convinced himself that the only relatives he had were Case, me, and the ones I had brought to the family. Despite being told, when he was seven, that a brother and sister had preceded him to Canada, he'd been too young for the information to sink in as reality. It was one more painful story that might have belonged to some other orphan. He had fleeting memories of numerous children, many possible brothers and sisters. He did not own a single photograph from his childhood. The most he could dredge up from the past was a blurred and upsetting memory of a woman lying in her bed, reaching towards him but unable to speak, the day he was taken away and put in the Home.

When Verna and Gordo entered our lives, they blew in like a singular pent-up wind. Once past the front door, they claimed Harry and he agreed to be claimed. What I saw was a large woman who introduced herself and shouted into the room, "It's our little Harry!" as she rushed forward. Their brother Gordo stood in our living room and wept. Harry did not drop dead from shock but his legs shook and he was forced to sit down. My legs were shaking, too, because of the excitement.

First impressions.

Harry, Gordo and Verna looked alike, a shocking surprise. From the side, their profiles were identical. I was married to one of what appeared to be triplets, each at a different stage in life. Harry was the youngest.

Phil said, later, when she met Verna and Gordo, "Put a toque on them, pull it down over their ears, turn them sideways and you won't know one from another. You won't even know male from female."

Verna and Gordo had been lucky enough to find each other when they were in their twenties. They'd been reunited in Alberta, the province to which they'd been sent as Home Children. Verna had lived on a farm near High River. Before the abdication, she'd even seen the Prince of Wales during one of his visits to his EP Ranch. All of this came out during our first meeting.

Both Verna and Gordo had moved east and eventually found partners whom they married, but they never lost their determination to track down their younger brother. They hit dead ends until Verna heard about and contacted an agency called The Missing Link. It was this organization that traced a path back to the archival records of the now defunct Home in England, and learned the area of Ontario to which Harry had been sent. Not long after that, three strangers claiming to be close relatives arrived at our door, unannounced, wild winds blowing.

As it turned out, Verna lived not far away, only a two-hour drive from Wilna Creek. She had owned a gift shop for many years, and sold her own handicrafts in a village close to Highway 7. She smelled of vodka and pepper, had a large body and a low, resonant voice. Arman was her third husband; she'd outlived the other two. Arman was younger than Verna by ten years, a chunkily built Russian with a thin beard. He had come to Canada by way of Hungary in 1956 and loved his new country. He was tight and muscular and was forever tucking in his chin and looking down at his upper arms as if he expected his biceps to grow while he was watching. From the beginning, I thought of him as a wrestler, or an outdated tightrope walker. But he was a travelling salesman for paper products, and frequently stayed in motels from one end of the province to the other. He told us that the way he stayed alert while driving through his territory at night was to talk to strangers along his route. When he passed a house or farm, he spoke aloud, as if he knew the occupants: "Hello, my friend. I'm passing by. I'm coming through. I'm entering your head." He talked to them about the events of his day, or about the sales he had made, or the quality of paper, or about music he was listening to on the car radio. Sometimes he said a short prayer, a blessing. This revived him and kept him awake at the wheel.

Having talked to Lilibet all my life, I understood.

While Arman was on the road, he collected plastic shower caps from motel rooms for Verna, so that she could use them as dust covers for seasonal crafts until it was time to display them in the shop. Verna was the same height as Arman, but larger. She called him "Ourman" in her deepest, lowest voice. She had picked up a hint of Russian inflection in sympathy with his native tongue, and she spoke slowly and deliberately, as if every word were a weight that had to be tested deep in her throat before it could be lifted out and used.

Arman was quieter than Verna, but devoted to her. He was also devout. The first time he sat in our living room, he stared at a framed photograph of a curved tree against a background of river and sky and declared that he could see God. He tried to explain the outlines to the rest of us—high forehead, large eye, bumpy nose. God was right there, hovering in the upper reaches of sky. Could we not see? But no one saw what Arman saw.

Gordo, Harry's older brother and the middle child, was a retired draftsman who lived in Fredericton. He was the same height as Harry, thin and angular. Twice a year, winter and summer, he made the two-day car trip from New Brunswick to Ontario, to visit his sister.

Gordo's wife had been dead for several years and, since that time, he had lived alone. He had a "nervous stomach," he told us, and was addicted to TUMS. Gordo had served in Intelligence during the war, and this affected the way he viewed the world ever after. He was alert but suspicious. He was also a man of firsts. He announced during his first visit that he took a bath the first day of every month, whether he needed it or not. He told us that during his first trip to the Maritimes, years after the war, he visited Shediac, where he ate his first lobster. He was attracted to the restaurant because of its design, a simple square building with porthole windows and an outdoor lean-to from which fried clams were served in summer. He had saved one bright-red claw from his plate. "I wrapped it in a serviette," he said, "and carried it out to the car. What a day." He added, sadly, "The claw is faded now, washed-out pink, but it's still on my mantelpiece. It was my first." Gordo fell in love with the Maritimes during that visit, and he and his wife moved there, and stayed on.

Gordo's peculiar arrangement with the world was that all objects outside himself were observed relative to the twelve o'clock position. This spatial orientation took getting used to. The first morning he woke in our house, he stood at our living-room window sipping coffee, and reported, "Man with yellow dog at eleven o'clock."

I knew he was talking about our neighbour, Pete. Winter or summer, Pete dressed like Paddington in a shrunken military jacket buttoned to the top, his bulging chest threatening to pop the buttons. He walked his Golden Lab twice a day. When Gordo reported the position of man and dog, Verna and Arman offered no comment. Harry and I exchanged glances. When I looked at Harry, I realized it would not be easy to think of him as Gordo's little brother. "This," I told myself, "is family. This is my husband's family, for better or worse."

After lunch—our new relatives stayed three days so that stories could be told—I served tea in the family room, which overlooked the backyard. Cardinals, sparrows and a pair of doves were at the feeder. Chickadees darted back and forth to the edge of the ravine. Gordo announced gravely, "Mourning dove at four." And then, "Danger at twelve." I looked out just as a hawk swooped down from the sky and scooped up a dove, leaving scattered feathers and pink blots on the snow. The attack happened so quickly, it was difficult to understand anything but a rage of flying feathers. I was certain the dove had died but, no, a few minutes later it limped back to the feeder. Maybe the hawk had dropped it in the snow. Maybe it had plucked up another bird in its stead and our eyes weren't fast enough to see. The dove's mate appeared, too, its chest puffing rapidly, in fear. I felt pity, to see the birds so frazzled, so afraid.

Later, we drove down the hill to the pharmacy so that Gordo could replenish his supply of TUMS. Inside the store, he whispered, "Man stole black comb, stuffed in pocket. Check ten o'clock."

Harry and I picked up the thread. "Gordo listening in at six," I whispered. And he replied, "Breathing space available at two." It was not hard to see that Gordo was lonely.

Despite the peculiarities, there was no disputing the fact that Harry was delighted to have a brother, a sister and a brother-in-law in his life. A ready-made family whom he loved instantly. Verna and Gordo, being older, had memories that stretched further back than his own. They knew details of their shared, early years in England before they'd become Home Children and were separated. Verna described their parents as she remembered them. Their father, she said, had blond hair and fair skin. We could not bring ourselves to speak of Matt. Not during that first encounter, though Harry and I looked at each other, panic-stricken, when his sister described their father and our son.

Harry invited the three of them back for Christmas, and they returned two weeks later and stayed ten days, right into the New Year. Before long, we met their children and their children's children, and after that there was a reunion every third summer, usually in our backyard overlooking the ravine. In one expansive shock, we welcomed fourteen close relatives into our lives. Case was introduced to an aunt, two uncles, five cousins and six second cousins whom none of us had ever known. Harry's family was bigger than my own.

Some of the photos Harry chose for his cache: Gordo, wearing a dark suit, Masonic sash and apron. When he met us, he told us he'd attended thirteen funerals the previous year, all Brethren, like himself. After our first meeting, he mailed the Masonic photo from Fredericton. He was standing beside his car, wearing a square apron with tassels and adornments over a dark suit. *Not navy, but dark enough*, he explained in the accompanying letter. Over one shoulder was draped a wide purple sash. I wanted to ask if the Masons' secret handshake was a myth, a boys' club in the woods. Harry said, as if he had known his older brother all his life, "Don't bother. Even if such a handshake exists, Gordie will never tell."

The second of the photos in Harry's cache was of Verna, her ample body being bounced on Arman's knee. The photo was taken in our living room. She was not shy about discussing her two earlier marriages, and Arman clearly enjoyed her stories. When I examined the photo, I remembered that she had been telling us about her first marriage and the honeymoon trip to Northern Ontario by bus to see the Dionne quintuplets. I pressed her for details, and she told us that there had been a long lineup, that it was a scorching hot day, that the quints' hair was arranged in careful ringlets. She had taken gifts to the quints, five barrettes shaped like butterflies, each a different colour and glued to a hair clip by herself. "I always had a flair for crafts, George," she said, her deep voice dipping into story. "I pulled the barrettes out of my purse and gave them to the ticket-taker, but I'll never know if the quints got to wear them. The ticket-taker was a real sourpuss. She probably kept them for herself."

One of the quints stared at Verna as if believing she might be her real mommy. Verna remembered that. She purchased a postcard before she left, and mailed it to the man who eventually became her second husband. The second husband, as it turned out, was a master pruner. After he moved in with Verna, he began to chop the bottom branches off trees in her backyard, leaving a row of spindly trunks and skinny-looking tips. When he finished those, he walked into the forest that was held at bay at the end of the yard and began to prune in earnest. Day after day, he pushed farther into the woods.

Verna said she didn't miss him as much as she had missed her first husband. "There wouldn't be a tree left in the forest if he were still alive," she said in her slow voice, which seemed to become more Russian than Arman's as she spoke. Arman snorted. He drew Verna onto his knee and bounced her considerable weight as if to some tune of his own. It was a sight, all right. Harry snapped the photo and it became part of the cache.

There were also photos of Case and Rice, Case at her theatre opening, Ally and me, Ally and Trick, our niece, Kathleen, who with her own family was now helping to manage the villa in Boca Raton, and Phil with Aunt Fred on Boxing Day. That one, taken the year Uncle Fred died, had also been snapped by Harry. The two sisters—both widows now—were sitting on the chesterfield in our family room, feet propped on the coffee table. They'd been listening to Mario Lanza, which Harry was playing for them on the record player, and they were showing off new mules, their annual gift to each other. Phil's were red, Aunt Fred's pine green. By agreement every Christmas, they threw away the old mules from the preceding year before unwrapping the new. A tinge of sadness can be detected on both faces. Although this is not in the photo, Aunt Fred whipped off one green mule after the picture was taken, and dusted the tabletop where she and Phil had just rested their feet. I remember Phil saying, as the record ended, mourning Lanza, "He died too young. I could forgive him his robust middle, but he died too young."

Aunt Fred was mourning her own husband. She had already begun to remind me of Lady Macbeth, not because she was an abettor or a murderess, but because she was constantly rubbing her hands. *What, will these hands ne'er be clean?* The line had been planted by Miss Grinfeld, and came to mind that Christmas, when my aunt's behaviour was painfully noticeable. I remembered the younger children at school running around during recess, dangling their hands in front of one another's faces and shouting, *"Out damned spot! Out, I say!"* and then running off, laughing like fools because they'd shouted the word *damned* with impunity in the schoolyard.

Aunt Fred missed the bawdy jokes, the passion, the daily battles with my uncle. She missed him until the day she died. And now, I miss them both. Aunt Fred died alone in her bed.

I gathered up Harry's photos and began to place them back inside the bedside table. But as I did so, I saw that I had missed a flat brown packet. I lifted it out and opened it, and inside were four black-and-white photos of our lost baby: Matt in his carriage, Matt held by a pair of hands next to a window, Matt lying on his blanket. The last was of Matt in my arms, smiling at the camera.

It was too much all at once. The grief poured out of me as if I had never mourned either Matt or Harry. I cried and cried and went to bed and pulled the covers over my head. I stayed there until the next morning.

It was only later that I realized there hadn't been a single photo of Harry in the cache. It was as if he had considered himself a voyeur throughout his life, looking in at his own family from outside.

I did not send the bedside table to the Sally Ann. The photos are still under the lid, there for the next person to find.

THIRTY-TWO

The floodgates have opened. Grief has no end; it only trans-
forms itself, over and over. Do grief and self-pity amount to
the same thing? I have to stop this, have to start thinking of
better times.

Harry and I were happy when we went to Europe. Not on
a grand tour; we made arrangements ourselves. It was such an
adventure to fly—a first for both of us. As we arrived in different cities, we booked day excursions or hired a driver to take us
around. Much of the time, we walked short distances or took
a local bus. When we made our plans, we opened the atlas to
Europe, sat back in our chairs and wondered at the possibilities—
the Somme, the Austrian Tyrol, Geneva, San Remo, Athens,
Rome. I wanted to go on to London, but Harry refused to return
to the country that had banished him when he was a child.

We ended our trip in Cyprus, flying in and out of Larnaca.
After checking into our hotel, we asked directions to the twelfth-
century church erected above the tomb of Saint Lazarus after
his second death. It was said to be the resting place of some of

his bones. Lazarus had lived an extra thirty years after his first death, and had been a close friend of Christ. Who would not want to see such a place?

The air was hot and dry the day of our visit and we were suffering from the heat. Harry paid the fee and we were handed two jagged scraps of paper. We jammed these into our pockets and slowly entered the shadows of the small church, all golds and blues—even the pulpit. There was no one else inside. We were cocooned, and could no longer hear sounds from without.

I saw a photograph of an icon taped to a table near the entrance, and looked up to see the icon itself—the resurrection of Lazarus. A round-eyed, angry-looking, mummified but haloed man had been partly loosed from his bandages. His eyebrows were fierce, his moustache angular and drooping. His arms had been tucked to his sides before he'd been wrapped—I thought of Grand Dan's cottons—and this made his revived body look off balance, ready to topple. So far, only his head had been freed. Strands of bandage flung out like ribbon-ends from his neck and his still-wrapped shoulders. The man who was unwrapping him wore an orange tunic, and was pinching his nose to indicate the stench. Christ was at the centre of the scene and, to the left, a group of brown-faced saints crowded the border.

I regretted that I had not seen this image during my childhood. It would have fed my own and Ally's imagination—though Ally would have redrawn the scene against a backdrop of snow. The nose-pincher provided evidence that Lazarus really did stinketh, as we had believed. I memorized every detail so that I could describe it when I returned home.

Harry found an entrance to a descending stone stairway, and I followed him into a black hole and felt my way down, step by narrow step, into a smothering, airless space. I had to duck to avoid bumping my head, and I paused at the bottom to allow my vision to adjust. I was directly behind Harry, and gave a shriek when I felt a bony hand touch my back. I lurched, realizing at the same moment that I'd been touched by the hand of a shrivelled old woman who had followed us down the steps. She pushed me out of her way even though, at full height, she barely came to my waist. She brushed past at a run—the distance was no more than four feet—and collapsed onto her knees on the tomb. Lying over the hidden bones, she began to moan and kiss the stone slab.

Along with adjusting to the moans, my ears detected the sound of a dripping tap, and this turned out to be holy water. Seepage from the tap dripped steadily onto the earth floor and disappeared in semi-darkness. There were no lights, but we became accustomed to the space around us and watched the kerchiefed figure as she collected water in a scrunched paper cup that she had picked up off the muddy floor. I was strangely moved by the scene, though the woman continued to ignore us. She sprinkled water onto the tomb and then a few drops over herself, and vanished up the steps as quickly as she had descended, leaving the paper cup behind.

Harry and I followed soon after, abandoning the world of the dead. Four days later, we returned home, our Big Trip at an end.

And now, here's a broad-winged crow, loping across the sky, listening to my story. A welcome sign of life. Is it the same crow I saw before? Have I been speaking out loud?

The sun warms my hands. I could break into "Zip-A-Dee-Doo-Dah" this minute.

I need someone to talk to. Don't go. Please don't go.

Fly away, then. See if I care. If you come back, I'll knock your block off.

I do. I care.

Caw! Haw!

One crow for sorrow. Two for joy. The crow is an omen, I remember that. Miss Grinfeld could not have foretold the lasting influence she would have on the crevasses of my mind. Or maybe she knew all along and planned it that way.

Cawing again. A dictator crow, warped and off-key.

Ha! Who calls? Bid every noise be still.

The crow saw me, I'm certain. It was black and sleek and on its own, which doesn't bear thinking about. Uncle Fred insisted that when you see a crow by itself it means bad luck—death or accident.

Stop dwelling on death, Georgie. If you do, you'll fall down and die.

I am down.

But you're not dead.

Talk to the living, talk to the dead, talk to crows. It doesn't make much difference. Maybe I'm losing my grip.

Harry and I half-joked about drawing the pillow. If he were to die first, I was to pull the pillow from under his head. If it were me, he would draw it out. "Not with a yank," he said. "Not with a jerk." It was a custom he'd heard about while living at the Dixon farm. Drawing the pillow was done to hasten the end and ease the spirit's passing.

I have no pillow here, though I wish I did; my head and neck would feel better for it.

I wasn't there to draw Harry's pillow. I wasn't even in the room with him when he died.

Leave it, Georgie. Pray, instead. Don't give up. Try the Creed again. Any line that comes to your head. Maybe you'll remember, this time.

Suffered under Pontius Pilate
Was crucified, dead, and buried

Death again. What I need is a good run to keep the prayer going. I prayed at rapid speed while flying over the ocean on our trip. It was a silent supplication, but my words kept the plane aloft: *Keep us afloat, God. Let us stay up. Keep us afloat, God. Let us stay up.* I alternated with the Lord's Prayer like beads on a rosary, the tail of the prayer running into its head: *Forever and ever, amen . . . Our Father, Who art in heaven . . . Forever and ever, amen . . . Our Father . . .*

I told Case about this after we returned home, and she shook her head in disbelief. She's a practical flyer. She willingly turns herself over to pilot and crew, and reads on the plane until she arrives at her destination. She isn't happy when fellow passengers pull out rosaries before landing, or cross themselves, or applaud enthusiastically at touchdown, implying that a safe landing was not expected.

Case, our childless child. Did our loss affect her so that she was unwilling to have a child of her own? We tried to protect her but grief lay heavily, even disguised. Now she has taken on the theatre. Her art is her child. She devotes every bit of love and attention to it. And she has Rice.

How I love my daughter, her infectious laugh, her appealing sense of humour, her beautiful black hair—touched up, now that there are a few streaks of grey.

I'd like to send a smoke signal—to Case, or anyone—but I have no matches. Why would I have matches? If I did, I'd probably set myself on fire. Now, having thought of matches, I crave a cigarette. I have no food, no water except a slightly damp sleeve and my own saliva, and I want a cigarette. Which shows how irrational my species can be.

There's a flurry over there. Black garbage bag at nine o'clock.

No, it's the crow, still on its own. Drifted down and I didn't notice.

Come here, crow. Hop over on your stiff little legs. I don't care if you're alone; I don't care if you're an omen.

If I'm quiet, maybe you'll stay.

I'm good to your fellow birds—though to be honest, not necessarily crows. One spring, we kept a watchful eye on a baby robin. Its mother hovered longer than usual because the baby had only one leg and teetered comically on landing. The mother guarded those abrupt little hops, that stiff-legged dance.

The winter Verna and Arman walked into our lives, they did a stiff-legged dance of their own. Sunday morning, they came downstairs wearing their bathrobes, asked to see our record collection, put a record on the stereo, and waltzed to hymns around the living-room rug. Harry lit the fire and then he and I—and Gordo—sat and drank coffee and watched.

They danced to "Tell me the old, old story," which could have been written for the waltz, and "When mothers of Salem their children brought to Jesus," which demanded a faster pace. Watching them dance to hymns we knew and loved cheered me in a way that I now find difficult to explain. I wondered, momentarily, what Grand Dan would say about my new in-laws waltzing to sacred songs on a Sunday morning, but she had been dead for fifteen years and wasn't around to offer an opinion. In any case, she had never smacked the bare bums of Verna and Arman; they were not part of her flock.

The logs crackled in the fireplace, the living room was over-heated, we were warm and snug, our coffee mugs in our hands. On that and every subsequent visit, Verna and Arman ended the same way each Sunday, cheek-to-cheek in a slow waltz to "The Lord's Prayer," belted out by Mahalia Jackson. After the last, long, drawn-out "Amen," they went upstairs and dressed and came back down and started the day all over again.

Harry and I were so cheered by this, it made me wonder if, like Gordo, we were lonely, too.

THIRTY-THREE

One photo I found after Harry's death was not hidden with the others in the bedside table with the hinged top.

The photo of the unknown woman.

I found it in Harry's wooden filing cabinet in the basement, the year after he died. I did not look forward to dealing with old files, and expected to find paid-up bills and old tax returns. When I finally decided to tackle the job, it was just as I had predicted. I spent an entire morning feeding paper into the shredder Case had insisted on buying, and which I'd set up over a wastebasket on the basement floor.

I did not shred the photo, which was tucked inside a brown envelope at the back of the cabinet. The envelope was in a manila folder, by itself, which gave it importance. It was black-and-white, five by seven, taken at a town dance. I knew this immediately, because I recognized the background, the suit Harry wore, and the tie. He had asked me to pick out his tie that night and I'd chosen a paisley mixture, which I knew he liked. The dance was held in the Lion's Club and sponsored by the Town Council to celebrate a fundraising campaign for the hospital's new pediatric ward. After we both dressed, Harry and I had a fight, a quick flare-up. Unlike Aunt and Uncle Fred—who insisted that they couldn't remember the reason for a fight when they obviously could—I have no memory of what Harry and I fought about, that's how negligible it must have been. Whatever the reason, I fixed him! I removed my party clothes, put on a housecoat, and stayed home by myself. He had to go alone.

Harry and the woman were standing back to back with their hands and fingers interlaced. Harry faced the camera full front. Most of the woman could not be seen; she was hidden behind him.

Who took the photo? Who enlarged it? Was a photographer present to record the highlights of the dance?

Harry and the woman were positioned in this odd manner as if they'd taken part in a bizarre dance routine and had to stop to catch their breath. Harry was leaning slightly, to accommodate his limp. The look on his face was one of not-so-secret exultation.

The photo was important enough that he hid it from me.

Oh, they were canny, those two.

Other details. She was wearing a long woollen skirt. Of this, I could see the hem; also, the heel of a dark shoe. I could barely make out a pattern on the skirt; it might have been tartan. She was shorter than Harry, no soft or bony shoulder sticking out. She'd have been thinner, smaller than I.

But who was she? Was it Jeannie Price, who used to work at the Town Hall? Anna whatshername who ran the hospital gift shop? They were both short and they'd have been at that dance. But their husbands would have been there, too.

When I came across the photo, I felt as if I'd been slammed in the ribs. Still on my knees before the shredder, I had to bend forward to place my palms on the floor so that I could keep my balance. My lungs were behaving as if my ribs had punctured them, and I began to take short quick breaths.

When did this moment of intimacy take place? What did it represent? I told myself that the photo must have been snapped immediately after a spot dance. That they were waiting to see who would be declared winner. But who was she, and why was she hidden in the filing cabinet?

I began to think of the woman as Anonymous-she.

Die, Harry, I said, after my breathing had calmed down.

But Harry was already dead.

Was this a matter great or a matter small? "Be not ignorant of any thing," Grand Dan had said, "in matters great or small."

If Harry had been alive when I found the photo and if he'd been lying on a pillow, I'd have yanked it out from under him. I'd have yanked it out hard. Instead, I picked up the photo, returned it to the brown envelope and carried it up the stairs. I opened the sharps drawer in the kitchen and slid the envelope under the carving knife. I tried to calm myself, closed the drawer, and took slow deep breaths.

I went to bed in the middle of the day and pulled the covers over my head.

Harry, I hardly knew ye.

Funny Bone

THIRTY-FOUR

That recollection ended in anger—or bitterness. Something unpleasant. If we were to see a tomogram of the human soul, would it show wedges of hidden spite, sharp-edged triangles of loneliness pushed up under the spleen, or tucked against the diaphragm and causing shortness of breath? Would there be barbs that jab at the brain and limit our insight, or that pierce the walls of the heart?

Stifle the bad parts, Georgie. Don't allow them to squeeze through.

I'm trying to stay warm. I'm moving, bit by painful bit. The sunlight teases before it vanishes behind a cloud. I could sing to the crow that flaps overhead. If I didn't know better, I'd think it was trying to deliver a message.

All things bright and beautiful
All creatures great and small
All things wise and wonderful
The Lord God made them all

Harry's favourite hymn was "Abide with me." He would have liked Teresa Brewer to sing it, but neither of us had ever heard her sing a hymn. I happen to know that he fell in love with the hiccup in her voice when she sang "Bo Weevil." That was Harry. His love for Teresa was something I could live with. Anonymous-she is another story.

I'm preoccupied with thirst, water being the necessity of life. But even though I'm weak, I'm not a bit hungry.

Uncle Fred used to say, "I'm so hungry, I could eat a horse."

A small potato would do right now. Served with a glass of water. Water is what I want, but a hot potato would warm me.

Celebrate the potato, Georgie. Imagine food, if that will keep you going.

Do you remember, Harry, the first and only time we visited the west? It was the year of the heat wave in Wilna Creek, the hottest summer on record. We had the travelling bug after Europe, and we chose the west coast because neither of us had been there and because we wanted to know that somewhere in the country there was cool mountain air. We flew to Vancouver and rented a car and drove in and out of mountain ranges, past the largest trees I had ever seen.

After British Columbia, we headed south to the state of Washington. We walked along the old market shore of Seattle, that beautiful city, and bought four yellow dahlias with flopping heads and carried them up the steep hill to our hotel. We inhaled sea air, took a ferry the next day, and I wrapped Grand Dan's shawl around me while we circled the Sound. The second evening, we walked down the hill to Ivar's and ordered salmon steaks and potatoes *au gratin*. The waitress was confused and said, "Do you mean grottin' potatoes?" and we nodded and looked at our laps. On the way back, we climbed the hill, and along the empty street

I found a black brassiere stretched out on the sidewalk beside a garbage bin, its cups flattened. A sad affair, I thought, and I picked it up and shoved it into the bin. I remembered it later when I took off my own before climbing into bed. We undressed in the dark and kept the curtains open so that we could look down over the lights of the harbour.

It was a hot summer on the east coast, too. When we returned, Gordo announced that he was coming for a visit. One of the photos I found in Harry's cache was taken at the end of that visit—the night of Gordo's only bath. He stayed a month, and went home the day after the bath. I kept telling myself to be tolerant. He needed cheering. He stared out the kitchen window at the chokecherry for long periods, and sucked on TUMS. When clouds swept over the house, he announced, "That puts the kibosh on that!"

In the photo, Gordo is wearing a burgundy dressing gown of flattened velour. Harry had given it to him, perhaps in gratitude after learning that Gordo had decided not only to bathe, but to return to New Brunswick. We were not sorry to see him go, but he was family and we put up with him. The night before his departure, Harry and I made love noisily in our bedroom, next to the spare room. I'm ashamed of it now, because we did it to drive Gordo away. That was not a magnanimous gesture.

But making love is. Harry used to say to me, after sex, "It's written all over your face. Everyone will know as soon as you set foot out the door." And when I went out, I felt strangers staring.

The moment Gordo drove away, I went straight to the living room and flopped down on the chesterfield. I listened to Django's "Solitude," all mellow and scrambly. He made it sound easy. He made it sound blessed.

The mind tricks. I smell river, though it's two miles from here. I feel mist on the back of my hands, and lick it off and remember the smooth-stoned shore where Ally and I used to go as children. The place has been called a beach in recent years but, name or no name, it's always been the same spot, a sheltered cove where the water is deep enough to swim. If you follow the creek far enough after you walk past Mott's old property—now a subdivision—you will reach the river. Ally and I sometimes walked there on a Sunday afternoon during the war years, when we were in our teens. We lay in our swim-suits, toasting ourselves on flat rocks in the sun. We talked lazily, in low tones, and turned back to front and front to back, so that we would tan evenly. When we were home again, we slapped gobs of Noxema on each other's back, cold splashes of white cooling our red-hot skin.

A few months before Case was born, Harry arrived home after work on an excessively hot evening and drove me to the river. Our old Hudson rattled a good deal and we bumped over uneven rock to a clearing on shore. As there was no one at the river when we arrived, we took off all our clothes and draped them over the grille on the nose-shaped hood, and waded in. The river was clear and swift and the water bubbled. I stood in cool water up to my neck and became part of the soothing current, and I swam. When we waded to shore, I wondered if someone would come along before we had time to get dressed. I was pregnant, and my skin was as soft as it would ever be. I was twenty-two years old. Harry told me I was beautiful, and I listened to old England in his voice and believed him.

Harry, my old love. I'm doing my best to warm up and stay alive. I'm even trying to celebrate our history. Hoist yourself up from the spirit world and nudge someone onto the downward path. I'm on my back in Spinney's Ravine. We walked here so many times, I won't insult you by giving directions. I rolled the car, Harry, the black car you bought from a salesman with white shoes. It landed on its wheels, though how that happened is a mystery.

I still think of it as your car and I always will.

I flew through the air, something I'm not proud of. I might have had banal thoughts as I flew. But there was a fleeting moment of insight. *I am this, I am that.* Flip sides. Joy or pain. Tears or laughter. Sink or swim.

Live or die.

I'm not ready to die.

Come on, you old bone. I'm cold and I'm old and I'm at the bottom of the ravine and my limbs are connected but I don't know how long I can hold out. I've sung and ranted and remembered our history and sent messages and prayed to God, and I'm this close to home. The home where you were beside me at every turn, good or bad.

I want to be heard, Harry. The way I was heard when we once whispered secrets at night. Your arm around me, my cheek resting against your shoulder. Last moment of clarity before sleep. In our youth, I carried your love bites on my thigh, your rapid heartbeat against my breast.

There's something comforting about talking to the dead. There is that to be said.

THIRTY-FIVE

All that from one small potato. I was trying to think of warmth; I was trying to celebrate food.

Here, then, is a celebration of food, sprung from the mind of Georgina Danforth Witley, who is trying her best not to be depressed.

Dumplings that melt in the mouth, plumped up and served with gravy.

Creamed peas on toast. Made with fresh cream. Stolen peas, if necessary.

Tea. A single, steaming cup.

"Let me hot up your tea," Aunt Fred said, when she topped up a cup. She poured Uncle Fred's directly into his saucer, like a cat's. Their youngest son once gave them a mug which, when boiling water was added, revealed the torso of the Pope. As the sides heated, the Pope's face appeared, his arms stretched open above a ridge of painted mountains. The Pope in the mug was the last Pope, the one who died. He's been replaced by Benedict—but I believe Benedict suffers from a touch of pomp.

He was elected to his new job at a ripe old age, which made me feel I should go right out and look for work. Like Lilibet and me, the Pope was an April baby, but I read that he was born a year later.

I'm older than the Pope. And I am lying here on the ground, while he is doing something with his life.

I'll think of water again. A tall glass. A cup, a flask, a jug. A creek, a stream, my body floating, head turning side to side when I wish to drink. The water is clear. I am not cold. I simply float and drink, float and drink.

Is that movement? The crow again? There must be other creatures, ground creatures all around. Do they keep their distance because I mutter and chant and sing to myself?

But the movement isn't the crow. It's a black garbage bag, a real one this time, snagged by a low branch. When I look towards the bushes, I see a dark shadow the shape of a long, sleek animal with a flowing tail. Is my vision clouding again, or am I deceived by the angle of fading light? At least I'm not seeing black spots any more.

What would Lilibet do if she found herself on the ground at the bottom of a ravine? No blanket to cover her, no Philip to wonder why she hasn't joined him for tea.

Is it true, Lilibet, that you and Philip have separate bedrooms? Does no one keep you warm under the blankets at night? If you only knew how lonely it can be after your husband dies, you might reconsider.

Could you stay alive in my circumstances? I never learned survival techniques. Unlike you, I was neither Sea Ranger nor Guide. Still, I'd like to know what you would do in my place, though it's not a practical question. It's a privilege of Royalty to have a chauffeur, a retinue following behind. But you know how to drive; I saw the war photos when we were young. You were still a princess and it was almost the end of the war and you were taking a vehicle-maintenance course. I read about you in the magazines, and saw you at the movies on a black-and-white newsreel before the main feature, which was also black-and-white. You appeared alert and patriotic in your uniform, as if you were glad, so very glad, to be part of the war effort. I was envious because I had not yet learned to drive, though I'd stood on a running board or two.

There's that flutter again. The garbage bag has taken the shape of a goose. I'm hallucinating. I'll have to think of food again. I'm in too much pain to imagine water. Every sound I make comes out as a croak. When we were on our trip, I sat on the end of the bed in our hotel room in Switzerland while Harry was in the shower, and I watched a black-and-white documentary on French TV. It was about the raising of a goose for the purpose of making *foie gras*. Harry missed the documentary. After watching, I was sorry I hadn't missed it too. It began with a French farmer proudly displaying his imprisoned goose, a bloated fowl stuck in a crate that had slats across the top. The goose's head and part of its long neck protruded up through an opening between slats. At feeding times—and these were frequent—the farmer poked a funnel down the gullet of his captive and poured corn through it. The idea was to force-feed the goose so that its liver would enlarge abnormally. Poor goose, its head stretched to the sky, throat extended, food crammed down its esophagus. I gagged on its behalf. It was not able to draw its head back down into the cage, and gave one loud croak. Is it any wonder that I've never eaten pâté since?

Towards the end of the documentary, the connoisseurs were not so squeamish. Four men sat around a rough wooden table in the shade beneath an arbour, and dipped chunks of bread into small dishes of pâté set before them. They sipped red wine between samplings. The goose was no longer in the picture.

That's enough to banish anyone's appetite.

There was another kind of goose, and that is better to think about. It was late spring, and we were on the Trans-Canada Highway, returning home after driving east to visit Gordo. Harry was at the wheel and we'd crossed the border from New Brunswick into Quebec. We were past St-Louis-du-Ha!Ha!, maybe even past Rivière-du-Loup, close to the St. Lawrence River. I looked up through the window and saw that the sky was filled with a mass of moving white. It was a few moments before I understood that we were directly under a migratory path and were witnessing a momentous, annual gathering of snow geese. Wave after wave, line after line, weaving and fluttering, down they flew, black wingtips flashing, white underbellies sinking to the dark earth of the fields. Every field as far as I could see was covered in strutting white. As populated as the fields became, so did the migration continue above. In the sky, tattered waves of geese buoyed up, drifted and sank. The weary fowl kept coming and coming, landing in fields on both sides of the highway. We stopped the car, and saw that other cars were stopping too. Truck drivers lined up their transports end to end along the shoulder, and some of the drivers walked beside their vehicles, pooling in small groups, speaking in awed tones and pointing to the sky. We got out of the car, and stayed where we were.

The scene made me want to fall to my knees.

Now that was a celebration.

THIRTY-SIX

We were good travellers, Harry and I, despite starting late. In Europe, we flew to Italy after Geneva. The paved hills along the Riviera were disappointing, but I was attracted to San Remo, our destination. We had a short flight to Nice and on the plane an attendant served tea with two cookies. I watched a tall man across the aisle remove every raisin before eating his cookies. It took him most of the trip to pick out the raisins, one by one. I thought of Case, who liked "rinkies" in her Cream of Wheat when she was a child. I looked back at the man just as the second cookie went down his gullet, and we landed.

The French and Italians had poured cement over what once must have been beautiful slopes overlooking the sea. Miles of greenhouses with flowers cascading down could not atone for the hills of cement that I saw from the window during our long taxi ride. But when we arrived, I loved San Remo to the last detail, starting with the sign on our hotel room door. *In case of fire, behave yourself as follows: If smoke makes the gangway*

*unpracticable, enter again your room, close well the door and show
yourself at the window.*

Harry and I behaved ourselves as follows. We fastened the
chain across the door, removed our clothes and slipped between
the sheets. Late in the afternoon, we walked the streets to take
our bearings. Flowering trees were lascivious to the point of
outrage. We entered a park close to the Ligurian Sea and looked
out at an azure haze. Trees sent ropes of vines down into the
earth. Magpies foraged while unseen birds hid behind giant
leaves and mewed like sideways-speaking cats. As we left the
park, a man hitched up his crotch. The varieties of public tes-
ticular behaviour in Italy could not be ignored. We carried on
to the marina and strolled past yachts, while small birds flitted
from the underbellies of umbrella-shaped trees. We returned
to our hotel and stood on the balcony and looked out through
the tips of tossing palms. In the early evening, we went for a
long, slow swim in the green-blue waters of the sea.

Our second evening, our leg bones were strong enough to
climb up into the old town. We wandered hilly streets, in and
out of ancient tunnels that had been carved from the moun-
tainside. We dined at an outdoor restaurant, starting with a
dish of olives, *pane*, and a glass of perfect wine.

At night, we slept behind closed green shutters. A giant
daddy-long-legs picked its way across broad tiles. Ours was
a corner room, our bathroom window level with an outside
walkway. I washed in the stone shower and heard a German
voice, a woman speaking while performing her ablutions, her
soft voice interrupted by the intimate voice of a man. They
spoke with comfortable silences between, as if they'd been married a long time, even though their voices were young. I could

have pushed open a shutter and stepped over the sill and into their company. When I came upon them later in the hall, I was surprised to see that they were our age, Harry's and mine.

When we finally returned to Canada, it was with a sense of newness that I walked through our house, opening windows, pulling back curtains. Isn't it amazing, I thought, that we so recently travelled roads we'll never travel again, ate foods we'll never eat again, visited sites we'll never see again. We've encountered people of a different history, a different destiny. And yet, we're back in our ordinary home and will fall into ordinary existence—for I could see that this would happen, within moments. I picked up a letter from the pile of mail Case had brought in while we were away. I made tea in my Brown Betty and placed it on a trivet; I looked out the window at the trees that had been on the edge of the ravine before we left and were still there when we returned. Harry and I lived lives parallel to all of those people to whom we had been momentarily connected, but would never see again. Individual faces quickly faded, but I've always been distantly aware of those continuing lives.

I'm so chilled. I must rest, must rest.

Where, twisted round the barren oak,
The summer vine in beauty clung,
And summer winds the stillness broke, —
The crystal icicle is hung.

Longfellow. There are no icicles above, but cold within and around. What if I get pneumonia while I'm lying here? Case ended up having it twice during childhood. Maybe she had weak lungs, that's what people used to say. I was fortunate to

have Grand Dan in the background once more. She wrung
out sponges of tepid water and laid them on Case's skin and
brought down the fever. She made us feel calm because she had
the air of one who knew what she was doing. I hope she knew
how much she meant to us. To me. I hope I told her. Not that
she wanted thanks or praise; she wanted none at all. But I loved
her and so did Harry. She had become his grandmother, too.

Thinking of Grand Dan makes me determined to reach the
car. It might take another day and night, or two days and two
nights—but surely, by then, my rescuers will be here.

I have the will. The sky is hazy but an outline of sun promises to break through enough to warm me. And look how I can
raise my head! I see a lump near the car, a streak of orange. Has
it been there all along?

I now know what a slug faces when journeying the forest
floor. I watched one once as it inched its way across the width
of our campsite, stuck out in the open all the way. It travelled three days before getting from one side to the other. We
camped a few times, when Case was a child. Drove to a wilder-
ness park and pitched a tent in a clearing by the woods and
pounded in pegs. Every morning when I woke, I checked the
position of the slug. Every evening at bedtime, I did the same,
using a flashlight. I did not want to step on it, but neither did
I want to divert it from its journey.

Harry and I knew every trail, every flower in this ravine.
Jack-in-the-pulpit—the bog onion—was his favourite. We
once tried to hike down the path in winter, but the snow was
crusty and the trail had disappeared. Each of us carried a ski
pole so that we could dig its pick into the snow to stay upright.
A third of the way down, we stopped because the footing was
treacherous and we were slipping and sliding. We stood on

the path and listened to the hollow sound as the tips of trees knocked together. We picked our way up the hill like defeated mountain climbers in reverse, scaling the slope towards home and our own backyard.

THIRTY-SEVEN

*H*aw! Haw!

The crow laughs. My sole companion on this journey. Though the dead are all around me.

Caw! Caw!

It bobs on the pine, is drawn to the tallest tree, hops to a short branch that is bare of needles. It fusses, hops higher and stills. It bobs its head again, makes a plaintive *Tchweet* and stares straight ahead. Does it see my rescuers?

I believe I've been sleeping. It's useless to tell myself I need water. Think of Aunt Fred. The rubbing of hands turned to repeated washing—*Wash your hands, put on your nightgown; look not so pale!* Oh, it was a thorough waste, her obsession, all that water going down the drain. But it was a ritual she was compelled to act out. I sometimes wondered if it had to do with Uncle Fred holding their sons' heads under the pump. Maybe Aunt Fred didn't agree with the punishment but did not object strenuously enough. The pump water didn't seem to do my cousins any harm. They turned out to be normal human beings like anyone else. All retired now, shoe salesman, roofer, banker. Though now that I think of it, the fourth became a dowser, a water diviner, and suffers from ulcers. And so life goes on.

After Uncle Fred died, Aunt Fred began to return more frequently to Wilna Creek. Because Uncle Fred had worked for the railroad, she had a lifetime pass to ride the trains. Phil cautioned me that Aunt Fred's doctor had advised the four sons to keep quiet about the handwashing. They'd been told that to bring attention to the ritual would cause it to get worse. When she visited, we were expected to keep a supply of soft towels and lotion at hand, to help prevent her skin from breaking down. The son who was the shoe salesman phoned Phil to pass on the advice. We did what we were told, ready to support. But Aunt Fred surprised me one day. She looked up from the sink where she was running cold water over her fingers—which had become stiff and red and raw. She turned off the tap and said sadly, "You know, Georgie, having to do all this handwashing is enough to make me weep. Maybe I did things badly and have to atone."

She still liked to come at Christmas and Thanksgiving, but she arrived the day after each holiday, after she'd already celebrated with the families of her sons. Before Ally moved, we took turns picking her up at the station. "Dark meat arriving," we told each other on the telephone. "Dark meat arriving on the train."

I wish Aunt Fred were around now. I used to phone her every couple of weeks and listen while she talked about her sons and their wives. When the conversation slowed, she said, "Well, that's it. That's all there is to report. Nothing much." She did tell me on the phone that Uncle Fred's spirit sometimes came to sit on the edge of their bed. She could see the depression in the blankets and feel the mattress sink under his weight. At the moment of his death, she told me, they had held hands, ring fingers touching. His last words were, "Do you see, Freddie? Over there." She turned to look but saw nothing except the dresser pushed against the wall. When she turned back, the tempestuous love of her life was gone.

My entire body is stiff, no matter how much I try to move. I'd like to have Grand Dan's shawl, fringeless or not. I could pull it over my head and that would help. I'd feel safe, comforted. My rescuers would find me wrapped in a black shroud. But there is little comfort here. I'll be swallowed by the root and no one will ever know I've been in the ravine. Branches will send out shoots from my limbs, foliage will spring from my bones.

Why do I think of the kitten that died for its trouble after crawling out of the creek? Everything seems sad. The universe is not in order. There must be something I can laugh at. I'm damaged, hard-pressed to conjure, too weak to envisage laughter. Can't swallow the image right now.

Nonetheless, laughter is necessary to our species. It keeps us alive longer, or so I've been told.

Knock, knock. Who's there?

It's the Happy Gang!

Well, come on in!

How naive we were. A separate radio world existed in another, separate time. Thank heavens for the CBC. And there was *Fibber McGee and Molly*. Uncle Fred enjoyed that program, and so did Mr. Holmes.

Sometimes it's difficult to find people to laugh with, and that is the truth. Ally and I still laugh, even though it's over the phone. She's had her own gallery in Boca Raton for twenty-five years and says she'll never retire. She calls the gallery Snow.

"You wouldn't believe how many Canadians are down here, George. They don't admit it, but they miss winter. They drift through the door in December and January and February and clean the place out. My paintings make them long for home. I can't keep up." Yes, Ally and I laugh, though she lives far away. "There's still a place for you at the villa," she told me. "The groundwork has been laid. Even security is looked after. Last summer, Trick installed an alarm system that is fail-safe. We hired a cleaning woman, too, so you won't have to scrub floors." She paused. "But it will still be your job to set the table."

Yes, we do laugh. And she's become more modern than I. She sends e-mail messages to Case. How I wish Ally were here now, to drag me up. We'd laugh and weep in each other's arms. And then she would put a cellphone to her ear and dial 911.

I wonder if it's midday. I hear the long call of a bird, followed by *ptew, ptew, ptew,* as if it were spitting something out. Something distasteful that's stuck in its craw. Or maybe it's uttering a bad-bird oath. I'm somewhere in Elizabeth's kingdom, bird. Fly away and bring back help. This bruised and battered slug is on its journey—and that's about as far as self-pity will reach. I've survived eighty years—I might or might not be eighty; my birthday might or might not have come and gone. I am not planning to make my exit in a gully. And I stink.

Well, I'm the only one here, and the stink has happened without my compliance. I've already suffered the discomfort, the indignity of wetting myself. But what else am I to do?

"*Lazarus did stinketh,*" Ally and I read to each other.

One childhood summer when we were visiting Aunt and Uncle Fred, our uncle chanted:

Wherever you may be
Let your wind blow free.

Aunt Fred looked over her shoulder from the kitchen counter and said, in her nasal voice, "Don't ask him for the last two lines. And forget everything he tells you, before you go home."

She and Uncle Fred laughed, "Haw Haw." But Ally and I wanted to know. Was it something taboo? Anything to do with taboos set us off. We did not have to be told which subjects were forbidden. "*Verboten*," Uncle Fred said with a mock-frown. It was not proper to speak of one's bodily functions in our house, but such conversations were acceptable in his. I already knew that what I read in Grandfather's books about what happened inside our bodies had no connection with real family life. Outside, we pressed our cousins to tell us the end of the rhyme, but they'd been warned to keep quiet.

Well I stink now, and that's all there is to it.

Phil once told me that complete strangers approach her to report their bowel habits. I did not believe this until I picked her up one day at the Haven and drove her to the mall. It was a hot summer day and we were in the parking lot and she was pushing her walker towards the entrance when a man stopped us and asked her, not me, the location of the nearest washroom. "I'm a visitor here," he said. "My wife is in the car and has to go number two." He shrugged at Phil as if they had an understanding, and added, "When you gotta go, you gotta go."

I thought we could do without the details, but Phil took the request in stride and pointed to the end of the mall. She was used to this. "Give anyone of my generation two minutes, and you'll hear news of their bowels," she said. "Your generation, too, for that matter." But in keeping with her Edwardian upbringing, her own intestinal news is private.

I've made progress again, crow, in case you haven't noticed. But my chest feels dense and dangerous. I'm beginning to understand the pain that Harry lived through—died through. Sometimes I think he wanted to punish me because it was he who was dying and not I. But that is another story.

Did Lazarus learn anything after his second chance, or did he not? Learning is changed behaviour, but how shall we ever know? Have I learned anything over the decades—or do I keep treading the same pathways, pulling the covers over my head when the going gets tough?

I must not dwell on my sorry state while I'm waiting.

Waiting for what? Waiting for whom?

For Harry to step forward and draw the pillow?

For Godot?

They sat on the stage, those tramps. But went nowhere. Still, I laughed. At times in that play, I did laugh. And kept my eye on the other theatre-goers, to ensure that they weren't letting our Case down because of her choice of play.

At the Queen's Lunch there will be smiles and laughter all around. Do the washrooms in the palace have taps of gold? I'll never know. Nor will I know what wines Lilibet chose for our birthday, or if lunch was served on solid silver plates, or how tender was the beef. It was my desire to sit at one of the tables where, early in the day, footmen climb up and wear special slippers to polish the tabletop in preparation for the guests, removing every last mote of dust.

Or perhaps there are circular tables, with celebrants divided into equal groups. I'll have caused a shortage, an uneven number. Was this reported to the Queen? Did Philip lean over Lilibet's shoulder and quietly make a remark about the missing person?

Not knowing how missing I am.

ORBIT

THIRTY-EIGHT

There was a long period in my life when I did not laugh, could not laugh. When laughter finally did come, it had all the markings of sorrow.

Harry began to talk about death several months before his illness became apparent. Leaves swirled in the air behind him as he stood at the back door and told me he'd dreamed of a clock bursting into flames. He looked away. "It was a dream of elation," he said. "I felt elation from flames devouring the clock. It was the energy of all that burning." He stared up at our own kitchen clock as if expecting smoke to pour out of it while we looked on.

He might have been telling me that his pain had begun. Was I listening? Was Case? She hadn't lived at home for a good many years then, and was not around to see the daily signs.

Harry made a move to find a doctor. His previous physician had died, and he'd had no checkup for years. He had an aversion to the medical profession, and who could blame him? There was a new clinic in town—at the end of the north mall—and one Saturday after we shopped for groceries, he drove home by a circuitous route and diverted into the mall, pretending it was on our way. He got out of the car and walked towards the clinic while I waited. He appeared to be reading signs. When he returned, he wrote something on a piece of paper. I asked if he was looking for a tattoo parlour, and he told me to mind my business. I was joking, but that's the way things were between us after the clock dream. That's the way things were if the subject had anything to do with Harry's pain. Elation was not a factor.

The name Harry wrote down was Dr. Harcourt Rhea. He didn't trust initials, was old-fashioned enough not to want a woman doctor. When he booked an appointment and went for a checkup—I did not learn this until later—he did not report his symptoms. The new doctor told him he was fine. A month later, Harry collapsed to his knees on the kitchen floor. I called the ambulance and met Dr. Rhea in Emergency. We shook hands and he said, "If only he had described his symptoms earlier, Mrs. Witley. The history is everything, everything. He should have told me." He referred Harry to a surgeon, Dr. Labrie, who operated the same day.

Harry had a complete bowel occlusion, cancer of the colon. When I asked him later why he hadn't reported his symptoms, he said, "If Harcourt Rhea is as good as the certificates on his wall say he is, he should have been able to figure it out for himself."

Several weeks after surgery, Harry was called to the surgeon's office for a follow-up appointment. He asked if I would accompany him, a surprise to me, because he'd been secretive at every stage. I thought he might be too weak to drive, so I got behind the wheel and drove him down the hill.

It was the first week of December, and snow had been falling all week. The storm was over, but the temperature had dropped to thirty-below, a still, cold day. The sky looked as if someone in need of hope had erased a thin line of cloud to allow a slit for the sun. There were shoppers in town; the landscape was white; loops of garlands decorated lampposts along Main Street. I had shovelled a layer of snow from the driveway in the morning—the snowplow had done the heavy work—and as I leaned into the handle of the shovel, I thought: With what ease do we do such things in this land. Throw on a jacket, twine a scarf around the neck, stride through below-zero temperatures as if we've done so all our lives. And we have. We've learned to tighten an extra button, to be more careful of foot. But we get outside no matter how old we are and, if we're able, we shovel snow. No wonder Ally creates nothing but winter in her art. Whiteness is engraved like permanent hoarfrost in our brains.

Because of the slit in the clouds, long rays of sun began to pour through just as Harry and I approached the medical building. I felt encouraged for the first time in weeks. I manoeuvred the car around a massive hill of snow that had been plowed to the edge of the parking lot, and drove down a ramp to find a space underground. I did not want to park outside because I was concerned that Harry might lose his balance. When I turned off the engine, he looked at me as if the two of us were facing a moment of truth. He told me that Dr. Labrie wanted to discuss the results of tests and biopsies, including a biopsy of the liver. He was to be given his prognosis.

Harry was wearing his thick coat, but he had lost weight and the shoulders and sleeves were too big for him. He held a cane in one hand; I had bought it for him while he was still in hospital. We took the elevator to the third floor and, when his name was called, he surprised me again by asking me to accompany him to the inner office. "To hear the verdict," he said. That's what he called it: the verdict.

When we entered, Labrie was standing by the window and staring out at the hill of snow. He was a man of Harry's height but younger, in his fifties. Slender hands, reddish-brown hair, a jaw designed to store weariness. I knew the look. I also knew that if Ally were to draw this picture, she would prop a skull and crossbones behind him, on top of the snow. The slope of the snowbank would be shaped like a question mark.

Labrie's lips moved in a grimace and I thought of my father, Mr. Holmes. We shook hands and he gestured towards two chairs set close together.

"I'm here to get a clean bill of health," Harry said, and sat down. He tried to smile.

Labrie did not return the smile. The results were on papers spread before him. He was sorry not to have better news. If only one lobe of the liver were affected, he might be able to operate and remove it, he said. In Harry's case, the entire liver was cancerous. Unable to stop myself, I recited silently, *lobus Spigelii*. I hadn't thought of the anatomy of the liver for years, and was astonished at how memory could surprise me when it was least welcome.

Both lungs were also affected. Harry did not ask to see the chest X-rays, though they were blatantly displayed on the wall cabinet, lit from behind. Instead, as if compelled to act a part in a B movie in which he'd been given a role, he blurted out, "How long do I have?"

Labrie looked more pained than Harry. "It's difficult to predict," he said. "Three months, maybe four. I'm sorry." He wrote a prescription for pain and handed it across the desk.

I kept my tears inside. I watched my Harry, the man who had rounded the hood of a car to bring me flowers. I watched my once lean and healthy husband push himself up off the armrests to a standing position. He shoved the prescription deep into his pocket, shifted his weight to the cane and waited until his thinner, weaker self rebalanced. He extended his right hand and wished Labrie the best of the season. He thanked him, and I thought, *He's thanking him for news of his impending death.*

If only social conventions would break down. I'd have preferred to see Harry run amok, shout in anger, throw himself into the snowbank outside. He saved that for later. In Labrie's office, he bowed slightly and turned to leave. I wanted to hold his hand tightly, never let go, but he needed his hand for the cane. The other, he kept rigid at his side.

When we reached the elevator, he leaned, straightened, and shuffled. For a moment, I had an alarming flashback to the hotel in Syracuse, when his body weight had collapsed against me. This time, the motion was side to side, a dance, a soft-shoe. More of a rocking motion than a dance, but a soft-shoe nonetheless, performed with the help of his cane.

He smiled his old smile and I was deceived into thinking the moment would last. I reached for his arm when we were back in the basement, but he pulled away and walked ahead of me, aiming for the car. The legs that had danced on the third floor no longer supported him. This time, they buckled. It happened so quickly, we were both taken by surprise. But instead of falling to concrete, Harry took a short run—counting on momentum—and landed with his upper body slumped over the hood. He lay sprawled there, his head turned in my direction, his cheek resting against cold metal. He was smiling to himself and I knew it was because he hadn't needed me. He pushed himself up and held me back. With his cane stumping before him, he managed four or five Charlie Chaplin steps and inched along the side of the car. He opened the door and fell into the passenger seat. His entire body was shaking.

I wish the day had ended there. But Harry wanted his prescription filled, and insisted on stopping at the pharmacy.

"Let me drop you off at home first," I said. "It won't take me a moment to come back down the hill."

But it had to be done that minute. He barked, "Pull over, park here, stop, oh stop the damned car. Go and get the pills and tell them to hurry up."

I had to talk to myself to control my fury. *He has a right to be angry, Georgie. Twenty minutes ago he was advised that the medical world has run out of solutions. You'd be angry, too.*

He glared through the windshield when I returned with his pills.

Compassion, I told myself. *Exercise restraint. Harry is going to die. This is not a contest of wills.*

When I started the car again, he shouted, "Where do you think you're going? Where are you going?"

"Home."

"Turn left, dammit, it's faster this way."

"I always go home this way."

His voice broke. "Why are you doing this to me?" And then he gave up. "Drive any way you want. I don't have the strength to fight you."

To fight me.

I kept hearing, *Why are you doing this to me?* The words had come out as a sob. It was the capitulation that frightened me. Even though he was fighting himself, the capitulation let me know that we were locked in. The two of us cried, silently, all the way up the hill. When we reached home, Harry went upstairs.

That was the way things were after our visit to Dr. Labrie. Each of us entrenched in separate miseries.

THIRTY-NINE

ZYX and WV
UTS and RQP
ONM and LKJ
IHG, FED and
C—B—A

Oh, there's no reprieve from living inside your own head. The alphabet sung backwards—of what use? Miss Grinfeld was obsessed with having us learn from every direction: forward, backwards, rote and rhythm. She placed the words of old poets in our young minds. Did she do transplants when we weren't looking?

But thank heavens for living inside the mind. Living inside a broken body gives little joy.

See how the branches droop above me. This is not easy to explain. The last time I looked, they were reaching for the sun. Was that when I first landed? When I first fell?

The fall of Georgie.

I feel silly, light-headed. My head has a hard ache. A bell

rings in the distance. I don't remember which day I left. Only that I'm to present myself at the palace on Wednesday. Oh, the grand staircase, which I shall never see. And I won't be wearing Lizzie's pearls; the case is out of sight, stuffed into a pocket of my purse.

Perhaps the bell tolls because I'm being mourned. Perhaps I've been missed and no one knows where to find me.

Leave them alone and they will come home, dragging their tails behind them.

One thing is certain: I am not lying in wait for the Grim Reaper. See how far I've come!

Be steadfast, Georgie.

Is that you, Grand Dan? I heard your voice again.

Have hope, courage. Push dig shove. Suck the buttons on the cardigan, even though there's no moisture left. Think of redemption, beauty, belief.

In Geneva, I stood in a museum that held Monet, Van Gogh, Cèzanne and Renoir, all in a single room. I didn't know which way to turn. I swelled and then shrank before them, and lamented that Ally was not beside me to see such beauty.

My jaw is stiff from talking to myself. My eyes are dry. They feel as if tiny logs are stuck inside them.

I need to get angry again. I need to make a hit list to pass the time until my rescuers arrive. Close to the top would be Harry, after our doomsday trip to Labrie. When we returned home, he went to the spare room, where sun poured in the rest of the afternoon, and he sat on the bed that had been made up for visitors. With his back to the wall, he began to read magazines, newspapers, whatever was at hand. When he came out of the room, I was aware of his fragility. I tiptoed around, afraid he would break, like an egg. He slept in our bed at night and I lay beside him with my gut clenched. When I got up in the morning, my gut was still clenched. I went for a long walk and kept to the edge of the hill because snow was piled high and the roadway had narrowed to a single lane. I didn't care if I slipped; I needed to get out of the house. As I walked, I thought about what had gone wrong between us. Harry had dug in, and he had dug in alone.

For days, he ignored me and stared out the window. He sat at the table for meals, but scarcely ate. He was in pain but could not trade the pain for words. He talked about it only once, and told me it reminded him of the flames in the clock. My memory darted and probed before I recalled the dream he had related in what now seemed another lifetime. Some mornings, I stood in the shower and cried without restraint. We could not move towards each other. Harry would not allow it.

Case gave me strength. Did I thank my daughter? She was part of this, too. She and Rice came up the hill as often as they could, even knowing how strained things were. They helped me to prepare for Christmas, and I was able to turn my energy away from Harry. Gordo was arriving from New Brunswick on Christmas Eve. Verna and "Ourman" were expected the same day. They wanted to spent Christmas with Harry. None of us referred to it as "Harry's last."

Determined to brighten the house, we placed red in every room. Case sat across from me and threaded cranberries. I thought of the kind of child she'd been, making sets, creating displays, always a flair for the bold and dramatic. We tied ribbons above doorways, ironed felt runners and stretched them over tabletops. Case dragged in branches of green, the way she used to drag in her "forests" for backdrops. I wanted to ask if she had said everything she had to say to her father, but I didn't. I knew that she had already received from him what Ally and I had never had from Mr. Holmes. Outside, snow was heaped higher than the windowsills. Harry became thinner as we decorated, but he was glad Case was there. He sat and watched and was cheered by the transformation of the house.

The day before Christmas, Verna walked into the house carrying a green basket made from paper and filled with crafts she and Arman had made during the fall. Inside were spray-painted pine cones, red-and-white striped rocks, lean, gritty-looking Santas painted red and carved to be bottle openers—Arman had done the carving beside the wood stove in his kitchen. He had retired as a travelling salesman, and had become Verna's business partner. I envied their closeness.

Verna had woven the basket from strips of grocery-bag paper and green crêpe, and she set it—now emptied of crafts—under the tree. She must have seen the look on my face because her voice drawled, "It's for your bathroom, George. For later. To hold extra rolls of toilet paper." Arman stood behind her and nodded, approving.

Gordo had driven for two days, negotiating heavy snowstorms all the way from New Brunswick. This dismayed me because of his age, but he did not wish to fly, he told me; flying upset his stomach. As if remembering other flights, he pulled a TUMS from his pocket and popped it into his mouth.

Harry was immensely cheered. He had his family around him. And I, too, was cheered.

On Christmas morning, Case and Rice had not yet driven up the hill. They were to pick up Phil and her companion, Tall Ronnie, from the Haven and bring them to the house at noon.

Because the inmates received so much attention, Phil had actually begun to enjoy Christmas mornings at the Haven. An Anglican service was held; gifts were given; carollers sang on each floor; musicians serenaded. Rice had done his part and had given a concert there the previous week, which Case and I had attended.

Harry and I got up out of bed and went downstairs. I made the coffee. Gordo appeared next, and the three of us sat in the living room with mugs in hand. Outside, the wind shrieked and tugged at the shingles on the roof. We were inside; we were warm and together. Not safe, but together.

Verna and Arman came down to the living room in their bathrobes, wished everyone Merry Christmas and put a record on the old stereo, which was still in working order. They began to waltz to "Hark! The Herald Angels Sing," and after that, "Adeste Fideles." Harry and I sat on the chesterfield and watched. It was the closest we'd been in weeks, despite the fact that we shared the same bed. I moved into his side, and the warmth of his body darted through me like a quick, sad memory.

At the end of "Adeste Fideles" and as if by prior agreement, Arman left Verna standing and went to sit in his favourite chair. Verna leafed through a stack of LPs, chose a record and walked over to the chesterfield. She tugged Harry to his feet. The two, brother and sister, separated for more than half a century and having found each other late in their lives, stood quietly until the music began, his hand on her waist, her hand on his shoulder.

At the first chords, they began to shuffle in time to "Abide with me," Harry's favourite hymn. It was Verna's gift to her little brother. His eyes were bright, almost feverish; his cheeks were hollow, his neck thin, his shoulders slouched. He was taller than Verna, and half her size. He limped while he danced.

Three months later, he was dead.

FORTY

Why didn't I rant and roar and rage at Harry?

Because of what we once had. I tried to preserve that, like a lone ember in a cold fire. And we did have something.

Harry died on the third floor of the hospital in the Danforth Wing. The naming of the wing was an honour belatedly bestowed on my grandfather, now recognized as one of Wilna Creek's pioneers in medicine.

What were Harry's last words? Case never asked—the way Ally and I had once asked Phil about Mr. Holmes. The truth is, I don't know if Harry spoke at all, to the nurses or to himself. Because I was not in the room when he died.

Just before one in the morning he appeared to be sleeping, and I went downstairs to stand outside the main entrance, to gulp in fresh air. It was March, early spring. I was desperate to be free of partitions and walls and the odour of Dettol. A strong wind had been blowing during the day, but had settled into a softer breeze. I wore no coat—only my Austrian cardigan. I stood in shelter of the low overhang outside, and hugged my arms to myself. I looked towards Emergency, the part of the hospital most brightly lit, and watched an ambulance pull up quietly, no fanfare, no patient to wheel inside. Two young men got out and I recognized them as the two who had responded to my call when Harry was admitted for surgery several months earlier. They entered Emergency by the same entrance through which he had also been wheeled on a stretcher in 1947, shortly after our polio honeymoon.

I leaned against the brick building. The town was quiet, the sky unusually clear. The stars seemed smaller somehow, as if they had shrunk inside their own shapes. There was still snow on the ground but it was spring snow. I had noticed signs of melting during the day. Honeycombed snowbanks were steadily receding; thick icicles dripped from the eaves and left puddles that turned to black ice at night. I wondered how long this would go on. There was no name for "this." It could not be called waiting. I was not waiting for Harry to die. There seemed nothing else to do but to come to the hospital every day and be with him.

As it turned out, I was in the elevator on my way back up to the third floor when Harry took his last breath. The time of his death was recorded as 1:25 a.m. A night nurse was standing in the hall and saw me step off the elevator. "I need to talk to you," she said, but she would not say why. She led me to Harry's room and put her hand on my shoulder and told me that my husband was gone. She did not say the word *dead*.

I don't know if he spoke before he died, but I clearly recall every gesture of our final conversation, two hours earlier. I've never told anyone about this. There had been no Cheyne-Stokes breathing, no death rattle, no farewell, no romantic declaration like that of my grandfather who had passed on the message, "Tell my Danny she'll always be the love of my life," before he exploded.

I had gone home for a shower and a change of clothes, and returned to hospital around eleven in the evening. When I walked back into Harry's room he must have heard my footsteps, because he turned his head to face the doorway. I could hear a distant voice, my own, inquire, "How are you?" as I entered. It was the polite inquiry of a stranger. A stranger who did not want to hear the reply.

Harry stared. He was propped against four pillows and he was so wasted, so unlike the man I'd once known, I had a sudden impulse to run to the bed to check his wristband to see if this gaunt figure truly was my husband.

He raised his arms, opened his palms and let his hands drop back to the sheets. He had no energy to reply. He looked out the window, to punish me, and his expression said: *Can't you see that I'm dying? Do I have to spell it out?*

When I think about that moment, I am confronted by the question I asked that was not worthy of response. Harry was offended. He was angry throughout his entire illness. He was angry until the day he died.

I did not pose the right question.

What was the right question? What did I want to say?

I wanted to put my hand to his cheek and say things great and small. I wanted to say, "Remember our good days, Harry? The months and years of good days, before your illness, before the pain?" I wanted to say, "Isn't it remarkable that two separate lives, our lives, managed to become one life."

It was too late. To say such things would have been an out-rage. Harry was going about the business of dying and he had gathered himself fiercely. Fierce was something I understood. I also understood that I was more alone than I had ever been. And Harry, too, was alone.

I had given up my anger. But was it also necessary to give up my love?

FORTY-ONE

After Harry was cremated, Verna told me what it had been like for her when her second husband died. She was in a confessional mood and we were alone in my kitchen. It was midnight and we had taken off our funeral clothes and were wearing dressing gowns. Arman was upstairs in bed, and so was Gordo. Harry's older siblings had survived him. Ally and Trick had flown in from Florida and were staying with Trick's relatives in town. Case and Rice had driven Phil and Tall Ronnie back to the Haven after the funeral. Tall Ronnie had loomed over Phil, and I saw how dependent she had become on his friendship. I watched him stoop over her as she held his arm and walked to the car. They leaned to each other as if they'd been partners throughout their entire, very long lives.

Verna and Arman had arrived at the church with several bottles of vodka in the trunk of their car. After Harry's coffin was escorted to the crematorium—that part was for family only—the two of them and Gordo accompanied me back to the church hall. They toted the vodka inside while I began to greet the gathered mourners. Gordo sat down, looking done-in and weary. Arman wore a two-inch wooden cross around his neck, suspended from a thin strip of leather. He had carved the cross from a maple in his own backyard. He had brought two bottles of Russian champagne along with the vodka, but the corks had popped while he and Verna were driving on bumpy roads and some of the champagne had overflowed. The bottles had been placed upright in a box, but were little more than half full. The vodka was intact, and was consumed in the church hall. The town had not seen a funeral quite like it.

The remaining champagne was left in the car and, when we returned home, Arman carried it in, popped corks and all. Verna and I sat together later, numbed by the funeral and by the leftover champagne, which the two of us had finished off. We faced each other across the kitchen table.

"George," she said, her voice deeper and more Russian after the champagne. "The reason I married three times is because I need to love. Sometimes I'd be sitting at my kitchen table, maybe gluing sequins, or weaving strips of crêpe, and I'd raise my head and say into the air, 'I love you.' But who was there to love? If nobody was sitting across from me, I went out and found a husband."

She looked at my face as if wondering whether to go on. "My second husband died making love to me, George. I swear it's true, though I've never told a soul. He never had a problem with his heart before, not a bit of chest pain. He was an out-door man, a master pruner. But he was passionate. You don't need to pass this any further but, well, he died the moment of—you know, orgasm. I didn't even realize what happened at first. I had to push him off. 'My God!' I was shouting. 'What happened! What's the matter!' I didn't know what to do, who to call. I would have to say what we were doing when he died. It would be everybody's business and the whole countryside would know. So I kept it to myself. I called the ambulance and said into the phone, 'My husband died in bed. Please come.'"

She started to laugh, and I laughed too, and we laughed for ten minutes. I thought of Grand Dan and her barked laugh at my grandfather's funeral service; I thought of the women of our family, hysterical in the front pew the day we buried Mr. Holmes.

Verna reached across the table and squeezed my hand. "Anyway," she said, between gulps and sobs—we were both crying now—"the forests were safe. The trees trembled when he came near, George. I wouldn't have believed it, except I saw it for myself."

The master pruner had been felled—not by a tree, but by love. It was a death Harry might have envied.

Verna went upstairs to join Arman in bed. Before she went up, she wrapped her big arms around me and said—her voice sounded strangely husky, like Harry's—"You learn to move on, George. You learn how to do this."

As I watched her haul herself slowly up the stairs, I understood that she had become a second sister to me. I thought of her sitting alone in her kitchen, raising her head and saying into the air, "I love you," and moving on. I thought of Phil, her mouth full of pins, taking up a hem—and rewriting her history. Phil had moved on, and now she had Tall Ronnie to love. I'd become used to Ronnie in her life; he, too, was part of the family.

It was late, but I knew I would not sleep. I stood at the kitchen window and stared into darkness, guessing at the outline of trees. I thought about Harry's last days at home. How

before going to hospital to die, he woke to find himself cling-
ing to the edge of the mattress. His body and the bedclothes
were so drenched in perspiration, we both had to get up so that
I could change the sheets.

I heard Verna's bedroom door close, and I went into the
living room and kicked off my slippers. I stretched out on the
chesterfield, still wearing my dressing gown. The champagne
was wearing off. I did not want to go up to an empty bed, so I
left a lamp burning low and pulled Grand Dan's shawl over me.
I stared at the ceiling.

I was suspended over rough water. Harry had sunk and I had
to row alone back to shore. We'd been headed towards death
for weeks and months but, irrational as it sounds, when his
death came, it came as a surprise.

Harry is dead, I said to myself.

"Harry is dead," I said aloud.

I thought of the third-floor nurses who'd been on duty the
night he died. After being alone with Harry's body for a few
minutes, I had been ushered into a small room off the nurses'
station where I was left alone to make phone calls. Case had
been at the hospital all afternoon and had gone straight to her
theatre from the ward. I knew she would be home after midnight, so I called her first, and told her not to come back. She
said she would phone Verna and Gordo, who had asked to
be notified, day or night. We decided to let Phil know in the
morning. The doctor on call came to the ward and did her
paperwork. I was permitted to wander in and out of Harry's
room. He was lying on his back. His body would not be sent
to the morgue until after I left.

But then I began to sense that the nurses wanted to call housekeeping to have the room cleaned and the bed disinfected and

readied for the next admission. I sensed urgency. Maybe they'd received word that a new patient was on his way. Conversation stopped when I walked past the desk. I went to Harry's room, lifted his cold hand and then tucked it back under the sheet. I looked at his face and, for a quick second, saw a crease above his right cheekbone. I imagined a loupe in his eye socket, held tightly to his orbit as if he were giving careful attention to some detail I couldn't see. When I looked again, the crease was gone. I gathered his belongings and took the elevator down for the last time. I stepped into the March air and felt as if I had been shot out into the night.

While I was stretched out on the chesterfield, I thought of all of these things—the nurses who wanted to get on with the next admission, Harry's cold fingers, his thin white body, the sheet tucked under his chin with the hospital logo showing above his sternum. I thought of Verna and Arman in bed upstairs, of Gordo in the room next to theirs, all of them now asleep. I thought of Grand Dan reading from Ecclesiastes and thinking back to a time when my grandfather had been alive: "If two lie together, they have heat; but how can one be warm alone?"

I tried to alter images that flung themselves into my head. Harry not moving. How could he not be moving? The wedding ring that matched mine being slipped from his finger and dropped into my palm. Harry beneath the lid of a closed coffin, the trip to the crematorium after the service, the reception at the hall with the mourners drinking vodka. Harry as cremains.

Would I be given his ashes in a box? Would there be small pieces of bone inside? Case and Rice and I were to go to the cemetery the following week, for the interment, just the three of us. The Danforth plot had been expanded to include the Witley name, and Harry's ashes would be laid next to our baby,

Matt. All of these things were going through my mind. I knew I would be exhausted in the morning, but my fatigue did not seem to be connected to the other events in motion.

I heard a noise outside the house, and sat up. There was nothing to see inside the room except the living-room furniture. *The wind is coming up,* I thought. *It's begun to blow through the trees.* What I heard next happened all at once, a loud but slightly muffled sound. Logic was not part of this sequence. What I heard was the sound of wings beating, many large wings marking time. I thought of the pair of doves that flew to the backyard feeder every day and I said to myself, *But this is the sound of hundreds. How can there be so many? Why would wings be beating at night?*

I thought of Matt and I knew that the sound was not from doves, nor from birds of any kind. Was Harry with our son?

Call me crazy, go ahead. I'm the one who was sitting upright on the chesterfield when the house was held, momentarily, in embrace. My senses reacted swiftly. I was immensely comforted and did not want the noise to stop. But it did cease, abruptly, and I was sad and let down and relieved all at the same time, even knowing that the sound was lost to me forever.

The next morning at breakfast, I sat with Verna and Gordo—Harry's look-alikes—and sympathetic Arman, who slid into Harry's seat at the end of the table. Far from being offended, I was comforted by the gesture. I asked if anyone had heard the wind come up in the night, and no one had. I said nothing about what had happened. I did not have the words to tell.

I would like to hear that sound again. The wondrous, all-encompassing sound of many wings beating.

The sound of angels.

Three

Skeleton

FORTY-TWO

Femur, tibia, fibula. Radius, ulna.

I'm desperate for water. I must have water. I'm closer to the lump near the car. Why do I so badly want to cry? I could cry all I want and there wouldn't be a tear to squeeze out. There isn't enough moisture left in me.

There have been times in my life when I've cried myself out. Cried until there were no tears left. For months, the carrot man was the only person I talked to after Harry died. Case and Rice came up the hill as often as they could. I attended plays at the theatre; I even volunteered at receptions for opening nights. I appeared to be a normal human being. But it was the carrot man I talked to. Going to the Saturday morning market was my feeble attempt to get my willpower working again. It was early summer and I told myself to get out and breathe fresh air, look at the world around me, start making meals again. I admonished myself for standing at the kitchen counter with a can of tuna and a fork. I stared out at the chokecherry, and tasted nothing. Sometimes a whole meal was a cracker slathered with marmalade.

What was I supposed to do? I'd slept beside the same man for more than fifty years. I was alone for the first time. Truly alone. I had been familiar with every daytime cough from another room, every adjustment of mood, every sideways step away from his usual behaviour. The months of his illness had been difficult, but I'd shared every one of those painful days. My life had been tied to his, long before his surgery.

I drove down the hill into town and walked past market stalls, keeping my head down so I wouldn't have to speak to anyone I knew. I did know people, but I nodded when they greeted me and they left me alone. I began to loiter at the carrot stall because, even when there was a lineup, the vendor, a wispy sort of older man with muscular shoulders, singled me out and began to take time to explain his produce. Dozens of carrot bundles were arranged along the top of his fold-up table. He explained how much moisture they required, how he sorted and priced and sized; how they cost a dollar less if I bought two bundles instead of one; how he dug a hole in the earth in the fall and buried them in a burlap sack so they'd last the winter months and into spring. He spoke with tenderness. He was never in a hurry. I loitered because he was a stranger and knew nothing about me.

How many new facts are there to learn about carrots? On subsequent Saturdays, he began to throw in extra information: what time he'd risen that morning to get an early start; how many years he'd had a market garden; how many times he washed the carrots before spinning and bagging—three. I began to believe that my skin would turn orange. Were carrots good for rods or cones, or both? Neither of us could remember. He was a widower, he told me. Did he pity me? Did I clutch my cloth shopping bag in a way that exposed my despair? If I had asked, he'd probably have told me that sorrow emanated from me like a scent. On the other hand, his future lay in carrots; he had dirt under his fingernails. He was speaking of loneliness. His, mine. I never learned his name. I drove back up the hill and thought of running away. But running away from what? Who was holding me back? And where would I run? I could not think how to plan the details, and suddenly remembered Phil running away from the Haven. I wondered how she had organized her escape—not that anyone had held her back, either. She had escaped without notice on a warm fall day, two years after she'd moved in. She lifted her coat from her locker, slipped her arms into it and pushed the walker out the side door. The rest of the inmates, including Tall Ronnie, were having afternoon naps. She began to walk.

It was Phil herself who helped put the pieces of the story together later. Old as she was, she had the necessary strength to escape. She still has. After I stopped worrying, I understood why she had left. I admired what it must have taken to make the decision. I marvelled at how she'd managed to get so far.

The reason she left was because of the *Wilna Creek Times*, which had run an item in the morning paper about a home for the elderly in Germany. A performing bear had been brought in to entertain and amuse the residents of the home. The bear was supposed to sit on a bench and eat fruit. Instead, it sat on the lap of a ninety-year-old woman and crushed her to death.

Phil was in the common room when she read this, and scrunched the paper into her lap. She began to laugh and couldn't stop. She laughed until she cried, which is what the women in our family have always done when we are upset. And then, she made her plan to escape.

She travelled back to her beginnings. She was not confused. She pushed her walker with the air of someone out for a daily walk. A woman who lived on a crescent three blocks from the Haven glanced out her kitchen window and saw Phil pass by, twice. She had gone around and around the circle by mistake. Hours later, when word got out that a resident was missing, the woman called police.

On her third pass around the crescent, Phil found an egress that hooked up to the highway out of town, a road she recognized as the old Wilna Creek Road. By this time, she was tired and discouraged, and she plunked herself down on the seat of her walker. Two men from the town Works Department drove by in a flatbed truck, rakes and garden equipment sticking up out of the back. The driver stopped, reversed, and asked Phil if she was lost. She brightened and told him she'd started out for a walk and had come too far. She needed to get home, and gave the men directions. They were happy to take a break, and hoisted her up into the back of the truck. They set the walker on its side and fastened it, told Phil to hang on to a chain at the side, and drove slowly so she wouldn't fall out of the truck as it bumped along.

"You can't imagine what fun it was to dangle my legs over the back," she told me later. She turned her head from side to side to show how she had taken in the scenery. "But everything on the old road has changed. Even so, the fall colours were glorious. And I saw geese overhead, line after line of them. I tilted my head to watch those wonderful wavering Vs."

After two miles, the men dropped her off at the place she

identified as home. "I wasn't being untruthful," she said. "The Danforth house was my home for a century."

"You sure came a long way, lady," the driver said when he lifted her down. "Good thing we found you when we did. Maybe you shouldn't go quite so far next time."

Phil thanked the men and sat down on the seat of her walker to let them know that she would stay in the sun for a while, in front of her house.

When the search began and the Works Department men heard a radio bulletin about a missing senior, they too called police. After she'd been picked up by ambulance and returned to the Haven and collapsed in bed, only then did she recount her adventure. I had been phoned and told that she was safe. I arrived at the Haven and sat beside her bed until she woke after a long, untroubled sleep. When she began to tell her story, I understood that she had been plotting for some time. She had planned every detail except how she was actually going to get to the house and back. The bear sitting on the lap of the old woman was the straw that decided *when* she should leave.

She had also not reckoned on the house being empty when she arrived, though she was glad it was. She took her time trying to reconcile the differences between what she saw and what she remembered. She pushed the walker into the backyard, caught the wheels in dead grass and stumbled over squares of cement that formed a narrow walkway from the door to a new opening in the stone wall. She found a crumble of stone that might have been part of our summer kitchen. Renovations had taken place and the house appeared to be smaller. Grand Dan's wagon-wheel garden was still there, but no rose bushes. How could everything change in such a short time? Phil was irritated by tangles of weed and undisciplined growth. She pushed her walker in circles, trying to remember where the chicken coop had been. She thought of her father driving the Model T that had given him so much pleasure into the tilting shed before he left for the war and never came back. She thought of Mott leaving cans of milk and cream at the back door when Ally and I were children. Then, she thought about the skim milk Mott had fed to his pigs and the skim milk that was served at the Haven, and she gave up. The past had gone and she hadn't caught hold of it.

She lowered herself to dry grass, took off her shoes, lay on the ground and slept. When the owners returned, they found her curled up next to the old stone wall. So peacefully was she tucked into the landscape, they were reluctant to wake her. The police were called for the third time, more than three hours after Phil had disappeared. By then they were already on their way.

FORTY-THREE

Well I'm not about to run anywhere. My bones won't move when my brain orders movement. The muscles of my arms and legs keep cramping as if they've been bound and tied in knots. I want these fractures treated! I want my bones set right! My face must be battered and swollen. There's nothing like real pain to clear the head. Though, admittedly, my head has begun to feel a bit foggy; I keep going in and out of sleep. Did I leave my bankbook on the table? Did I destroy the photo of Anonymous-she? Damn the cheese, going rotten in the fridge.

And now I hear the bell again. I might not be able to stand, I might not be mistress of my own fate, but there's nothing wrong with my hearing.

Never send to know for whom the bell tolls. . .

There is absolutely no point in bellyaching. Didn't I teach that to Case?

Maybe I won't mind so much, if the bell does toll for me. There's a bar that is crossed—about minding—though I'm not exactly sure where it is.

For God's sake, Georgie. Think of what you just said.

Well maybe I won't. I didn't get to choose the place, but I might get to choose the time.

I'm turning into a raving woman.

Maybe she's been inside you for a long time.

Maybe she has. Maybe I'm already dead. I'm weary. My skin is numb. There's a feeling of heaviness inside my chest. I can't feel my feet. I remember now, falling in and out of a dream in which I saw my own heart, my own mitral valve. It lay above a mess of carrot tops in a garden gone wild. When I woke, I had a moment's disappointment at finding myself sealed inside my own skin.

Who dreams of seeing their own mitral valve?

Someone who grew up reading *Gray's*, that's who.

The crow comes and goes as it pleases now; my presence doesn't bother it one bit. It flew low over my head and stared into my squinted face with its beautiful dark eye.

A crackling sound again, and this one's nearby.

Come closer. Please. Is someone there?

Don't then.

If you don't want to show yourself, then bugger off!

My God, what's come over me? Would Lilibet tell a living creature to bugger off? Not someone who owns all those corgis and dorgis, with their pert little fox heads. But she's had her problems. Her *annus horribilis* was more than a decade ago. Think of the ups and downs with Diana. And I felt sorry for her when I saw her priceless paintings as they were carried out of Windsor Castle, rescued from the fire. She was sturdy in her

boots as she tromped around the grounds in the midst of bedlam, looking as if she'd come from good country stock.

Still, somehow I can't see her breaking into a fierce yell. Does
she swear? Does she shout at Philip, or at Charles and Camilla?
Before the car accident, did she yell at Lady Di?

My own *annus horribilis* happened long before that. It's been
with me all of my adult life. Any bad thing that happened rattled against it like new memory whipping up old.

Whatever was moving has vanished, but I wish it would
come back. There's only so much a person can take. I don't
mean the crow; the crow flaps overhead, alone again.

One morning I looked up a word while I was doing my
crossword, and opened the *Oxford* dictionary to a page where
two words in bold print leapt off the upper corner: *bugger off.*
I was so surprised, I checked the entry, which also defined
bugger all. Gordo, Harry's lost-and-found brother, used to say,
as he stood at the window looking out at the chokecherry,
"Sweet bugger all."

Well Gordo's alive and I'm alone and Harry's dead, and that's
all there is to it.

Sweet bugger all.

FORTY-FOUR

Look where I am. I should be encouraged, but all I can manage is a desperate fatigue. Still, I'm in the open. I see the railing up there, the edge of layered rock—black-tipped like the wings of the snow geese. I see snapped trees hanging upside down, old vines that droop and swing. If anyone looks over the railing, I'll be seen. Maybe Pete and his yellow dog will come down the path after all.

Alleluia!

If someone is listening, please take away this chill wind that has begun to roll along the ground. Take it away before I lose my train of thought. The wind enters my left ear and shrills inside my head. That bothers me more than the pain in my arm and leg.

Do your ears hang low?
Do they wobble to and fro?

Uncle Fred sang to his sons, and to Ally and me. He sang

276

to Aunt Fred. He laughed at himself, never took himself too seriously.

Something distracting hovers at the outer edge of memory. Something I can't quite place. My thoughts are slurring. I must relate the things I know. I must think of Case. If only I had the chance to tell her what I know.

She's creating her own stories. She has her own life.

Still, I know the bones. I have longevity in my own. Grand Dan lived to ninety-five, and everyone who knew her still mourns her passing. Aunt Fred lived to ninety-one—even after all the handwashing. You'd think she'd have washed herself away. Phil will be a hundred and four in October. Does she manage to look forward more than she looks back?

I'll celebrate with her at the Haven on her birthday this year, or anywhere she and Tall Ronnie would like to be. Maybe Case and I can bring her to the house to watch a string of old Mario Lanza movies, or to the theatre, or a fancy restaurant. We'll take her wherever she wants to go. We'll borrow a wheelchair from the Haven and I'll help her into it and push her in any direction she points. The leaves will be blazing because it will be fall. Red will slip down over the giant maples like a sheath. We'll look at the glorious sight and sigh a collective sigh and give thanks for the unasked-for beauty.

I must hire someone to clean out the eaves in the fall. They haven't been done since Harry died. He climbed down the ladder every October and announced, "The runnels are clean." His cheeks were rough and reddened. He wore gardening gloves with wide flat fingers, the ones I bought at Home Hardware, so he wouldn't cut his hands on rusting metal.

Eaves and sheaves, same season.

We shall come rejoicing
Bringing in the sheaves

How difficult to sing when only a pale rasp comes out. Or maybe I was singing in my head.

Verna and Arman danced to that, too. They did an improvised foxtrot. And here's a leaf now, its rounded contours wafting down. Last year's dried leaf ousted by a new one, unfurled.

Verna told me that since "Ourman" stopped being a travelling salesman, he sits across from her in the evening and says, as if he's still behind the wheel, driving through the landscape of their living room, "I'm entering your head, Verna. I'm coming into your thoughts. Make room for me."

She laughs like a schoolgirl and so do I when she phones. I miss her largeness, her ample body spilling over the edges of my kitchen chair, her generous spirit, her adopted Russian voice—they're all a comfort. When I get out of this ravine I'll phone and invite her and Arman to come and stay with me a while. I haven't seen them for months.

And Ally makes me laugh. She wants me to come to Boca Raton. My beloved sister, she'll never stop asking—and it's good to be wanted. Maybe I'll go after all. Take up my duties at the villa, at last. Shake out the linen and set the table with Grand Dan's fine old silver.

FORTY-FIVE

Have I slept? I feel as if a weight has been implanted in my side.

I wonder if my body has left tracks where I've dragged myself, like the wake of a ship, earth parting.

You've had plenty of chance to lay down tracks.

I don't want followers. I don't mean that. I've tried not to be trapped in repetitive furrows of my own.

Who are you to escape life's patterns?

My limbs are swollen, so tender, it's hard to think of a reply. Admittedly, I dare not add up the hours and days I sat at my kitchen table and stared into space after Matt, and then, years later, after Harry died. Grief does that. It can't be warded off. It strikes like a steel arrow embedded in the bowels. One that can never be removed.

I did stare into space, yes, but that didn't add up to my whole life. After Harry died, I kept thinking about how I'd never become anything. The thought is still lodged in my head, a bone stuck crosswise in a shallow pit. Harry was a jeweller, a good one; everyone said so. Case owns a theatre; she has taken charge of her life and I am so proud of her. Rice is a musician; he makes my daughter happy and I love him for that. Ally is a painter and has a gallery called Snow. Trick looks after the villa. Phil was a seamstress. Grand Dan a midwife. Lilibet got to be Queen. The Pope has a job—he hasn't been in it that long. Verna and Arman will run the craft shop until they drop. Only Gordo stands at the window, staring out. But even he was a draftsman, before he retired.

And what contribution have I made? What is a life worth? I might as well ask. Have I learned anything?

Reciter of bones, lover of poems—memory has always been my long suit. Shelver of books. I once drew better-than-average lungs and a superior vena cava. A drawing that wasn't mailed. I created checkerboard sandwiches for family gatherings. I was daughter to Phil and Mr. Holmes, granddaughter to Grand Dan and my unmet grandfather, wife of Harry, mother of Case, my child, and for a short time, little Matt.

That is a good and worthy occupation. Raising a child.

And losing one? Did I wrap him too tightly? Did the blanket cover his face? Oh, I'll never get over it. Every detail of his little body lies cold behind my eyes.

What's done cannot be undone.

I threw the glass-leafed tree. I flung it against the wall and was glad it flew from my palm.

But you raised Case; look at the bright and compassionate woman she has become; you raised her well.

Then why is that period—the one when I was caring for her—why are those years so blurred when I try to recall? Events clump together; I can't single them out.

Maybe that's when you were busiest. Did you think of that?

I did not. But I loved those years. I feel a heavy weight of joy and sadness when I think of them. Joy because I lived them. Sadness because they're gone.

I have the right to stay alive, don't I? Don't I qualify? I tried not to throw my time away. What was I supposed to do with it?

I made good scalloped potatoes.

Don't depress yourself, Georgie. Think of the people who were nourished by those potatoes.

Maybe I didn't have enough determination. It's possible I attended to the wrong things. Think of Lilibet. After the abdication, after her father's death, her work was cut out for her. She was thrown into the arena, whether she wanted the job or not. But the job was already there; she didn't have to decide.

You could have been a doctor, like your Grandfather Danforth.

Don't taunt me. There was no money for medical school. I met Harry and became a wife. And being Harry's wife was, in its own way—it was at the time—a job. Until Case and Matt were born. And then the job became bigger, somehow. More important. But what was the job about? I need to tell myself.

I taught Case to love language; I chanted nursery rhymes; I sang, explained words, encouraged her to walk, try, run. And there were diapers strung on the line, rompers to smock, Harry's cuffs and collars to starch, tea towels to fold, Sunday roasts to cook, cheese biscuits to bake, layer cakes to cool on racks, school concerts to attend. Someone had to do those things.

Oh, stop. I amount to my own story. I am what I am.

I have to stretch my body. I must have dozed. I'm dim-witted. I dreamed I reached out a hand and touched something soft. I'm losing my marbles. Mistress of sequential disarray. An unnamed beast came into my dream and began to ravage the room I was in.

Shelves were knocked over. The tree fell; its glass leaves, its silk limbs lay on the floor. The beast could not be stopped.

I looked into the dark eye of the crow.

Death, you invade me. If I had any energy left at all, I'd tell you to put up your dukes.

Does the body give up all at once? Does it happen quickly? Maybe I really won't mind. I've never felt old inside, but the joints get stiffer, the bones do age. What is this I'm touching? Orange paper that isn't very orange any more, collapsed into dampness like something rotting. But something I can pull towards me. I've reached the lump, the package that rolled from the car when the door was sprung. Case's gift. She placed it on the passenger seat when she came up the hill to say good-bye. With my one good hand I can pull the paper away and see what's inside.

A shawl. A new one to replace Grand Dan's, which I've worn to a thread. I wasn't to open the gift until I was on the plane. It's indigo, thick and soft, will match the pale blue of my dress to perfection. Case, you wanted me to wear this to the palace. And here's your note on cardboard, buried in the folds of cloth, nothing fancy, done in a hurry—you're always in a hurry. You'll have to learn to slow down. I don't need my glasses to read this; it's bold, printed in black felt-tip: DEAREST MOM—YOU CAN PULL THIS OVER YOUR HEAD WHILE YOU'RE HOLDING THE PLANE UP OVER THE OCEAN. GIVE MY LOVE TO THE QUEEN. XXX CASE

Oh, my darling daughter. I can't keep from crying. I've got the dry heaves. It's the best gift I've ever received. I can pull it over my head, keep the wind from shrilling in my ear. *Structure determines function*, Grandfather. You'd appreciate that.

Start strumming, Django, something about the day is done.

I'll hear you, even with my ears covered. Can you feel the rhythm of my heartbeat, Matt? Oh, my loves, Case and Matt and Harry and Ally and Grand Dan and Phil. How we've cared for one another—in life and in death. And Rice and Trick and Mr. Holmes. Aunt and Uncle Fred. Verna and Ourman. Gordo and Tall Ronnie. The Carrot Man, Miss Grinfeld, Anonymous-she. It's easy to love everyone when you're on the way out.

What if Harry isn't there? What if Anonymous-she has arrived before me? I tried not to bear a grudge. I tried to make use of my chances, though I've squandered some. I did my best not to lie to myself, not to be ignorant in matters great and small.

I've missed my chance to meet Lilibet in person, though she did wave from the back seat of her limo. I hear my rescuers now. Haven't they been there all along—stick figures up above? Mouths moving as if they're shouting, arms waving over the railing. Figuring out the best way to get a stretcher down the path.

I can go, now. I know my skeleton won't rot in the ravine. Are you listening, God? I can't alter my compass. There's no use bluffing. I'm still not sure. I've had my life and it's been a privilege. It's a miracle anyone gets through.

Move over, Harry.

Case, my darling, don't be sad. Care for the people you love. Take back the shawl, pull it over your head when you . . .

ACKNOWLEDGEMENTS

For discussions along the way, I thank Frances Hill, Jean Stratton, Jane Anderson, Joel Oliver, Janet Lunn, Deborah Windsor, Donna Wells, Barbara Mitchell, Orm Mitchell, Dr. John Young, Brian Hill, Gwen Hoover, Cath Hoogerhyde, Faith Schneider, Bryan Moon for our ancient ramblings and fantasies about Turks, and Patrick McGahern of Patrick McGahern Books for swiftly locating a copy of *Gray's Anatomy*, 1901. For background information, I acknowledge delving into *The Home Children*, Phyllis Harrison, ed.; Hodder & Stoughton's *The Princess Elizabeth Gift Book*, 1935; *Queen of Home*, 1892, by Emma Churchman Hewitt; *Maclean's* January 15, 1937, Abdication issue; as well as various issues of *Better Homes & Gardens; Woman's Day; Chatelaine* from 1945, 1957, 1971. *The Ottawa Citizen* published the Queen's birthday lunch invitation as well as countless articles I have collected since 1994, about unfortunate persons who plunged over the edges of roads, cliffs and ravines inside their vehicles. The item about the German bear is from *The Ottawa Citizen*, August 9, 2002. The War cake referred to is from a vintage recipe (World War One) in J. Anderson's *American Century Cookbook*.

Thanks to Will Shakespeare for his everlasting *Macbeth* and *Julius Caesar*.

The epigraph from the poem "Relating" is reprinted from *Always Now* (in three volumes) by Margaret Avison, by permission of The Porcupine's Quill. Copyright © Margaret Avison, 2003.

Love and thanks to Sam and Craig for sharing expertise from your chosen fields and the outdoor world. Love to Russell and Aileen for sharing your expertise in music and music history. Thanks to the four of you for answering the varied questions I put to you. How blessed I am to have such children.

Thanks to Ted, who was there at the beginning, in Geneva, when *Bones* began in laughter.

Thanks, always, to my agent, Jackie Kaiser at WCA, for her hard work, friendship and never-failing support. Thanks to Natasha Daneman at WCA, on the international front.

Special thanks to the always surprising Phyllis Bruce, my Canadian editor and publisher, who—apart from putting her hands on a cache of Royal memorabilia—looked over the scattering of bones at an earlier stage and handed me, in a single word, the sinew. I much appreciate the suggestions, questions and discussions. Thanks also to the entire team at HarperCollins for the commitment and the great support—especially Noelle Zitzer and Nita Pronovost.

I thank Elisabeth Schmitz, my American editor, for her perceptive editing and invaluable suggestions. I am grateful for the strong support of Grove/Atlantic in New York and Hodder & Stoughton in London.

Any musings about the Queen and ongoing events at the palace are fictional ramblings of Georgie.

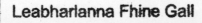